T0354964

FOOTPRINTS

FOOTPRINTS

A Collection of Short Stories

ROBERT CALLIS

FOOTPRINTS
A COLLECTION OF SHORT STORIES

iUniverse books may be ordered through booksellers or by contacting:

iUniverse
1663 Liberty Drive
Bloomington, IN 47403
www.iuniverse.com
844-349-9409

Because of the dynamic nature of the Internet, any web addresses or links contained in this book may have changed since publication and may no longer be valid. The views expressed in this work are solely those of the author and do not necessarily reflect the views of the publisher, and the publisher hereby disclaims any responsibility for them.

Any people depicted in stock imagery provided by Getty Images are models, and such images are being used for illustrative purposes only. Certain stock imagery © Getty Images.

ISBN: 978-1-6632-6345-2 (sc)
ISBN: 978-1-6632-6346-9 (e)

Library of Congress Control Number: 2024910913

Print information available on the last page.

iUniverse rev. date: 05/31/2024

CONTENTS

DEDICATION

This book is dedicated to my daughter Christine M. Arndt.

Every year for the past fifteen years I have drafted a short story and distributed it to friends and family at Christmas.

This year, Chris wrote to me and suggested I make a book out of all the stories I had shared. This book is the fulfillment of that suggestion.

A man is rich if he has friends and family.

THE REUNION

In high school, everyone had a nemesis. Someone who disliked you, and you disliked them. I guess it's just part of nature. Not everyone is going to like you and you are not going to like everyone. Sometimes there is a specific incident that created this animosity, but often it just evolved.

In my case I grew up in a small town and attended a small high school. The high school had about two hundred and twenty students and I knew all of them by name. I knew a boy who was a year older than me who made a sport of bullying me in junior high school. When I was a freshman, I had grown to just over six feet tall and went out for football. My bully just seemed to disappear into the rows of lockers that lined the hallways of the old school building. Of course, I had grown to be six-foot one inch tall as a freshman, but I only weighed about 126 pounds.

Although my high school class had cliques like any other school, kids still socialized outside of their cliques. I knew the kids I hung out with better than any other kids in my class. I lettered in football, basketball, and track in high school, which was a small school, and that extended my circle of friends.

To be truthful, I was a lousy student. I was interested in

sports, cars, and girls, in that order. School and studying did not make my top ten list. I graduated 33rd in a class of sixty-six. You can't get any closer to the upper 50% of your class than that. I also worked at a gas station and my stepbrother's clothing store. Like many high school students, I couldn't see the future beyond the end of my nose.

There were a couple of guys in my class that I didn't much care for, but I simply avoided them for the most part and things went fine. That is until the spring of my junior year. It was late in the afternoon, and I ran into my current girlfriend. She told me she had something important to tell me. I stopped and listened. She told me five junior boys had been selected for Boys State. I knew about this but had little or no interest in Boys State and knew almost nothing about it.

She went on to say she heard one of our male classmates, who was selected for Boys State, telling a group of our classmates the reason I was not selected for Boys State was because I hung out with a rough crowd. Now, I really didn't give a hoot about Boys State until then. I wasn't interested, had not been selected, and this guy I did not care for had been selected. He's going and I'm not. He won, or whatever. But the fact that he decided to portray me as some sort of juvenile delinquent and unworthy of Boys State really pissed me off.

I was mad, and it showed. I related the story to two of my best friends. Both of whom were from the same rough crowd I was associated with. It was the end of the school day, and I was headed down to the locker room to get ready for track practice with both of my friends following close behind. They were hoping for some form of violence because I rarely got mad. They were sure violence was on the upcoming agenda, and they didn't want to miss it.

When I entered the locker room, it was already almost full of guys getting dressed for track practice. The guy I was looking for was not on the track team. He did play football and the football team went out for track just to keep in shape and to keep the football coaches happy.

I headed down the row of lockers where I knew I would find my quarry. Sure enough, he was just taking off his shirt in front of his locker. He saw me coming, and he saw my two friends trailing behind with big smiles on their faces. As I walked up to him, I could see the fear in his eyes. He actually backed himself up against his locker as I confronted him.

I said, "Congratulations on being selected for Boys State" and stuck out my hand. His eyes were now full of shock, and he slowly extended his hand for me to shake. I shook it and moved past him to the next row where my locker was located. Both of my friends followed me and when we were out of sight, they both broke up in laughter.

I never trusted that skunk again. In a football game that next fall, I was a running back and my nemesis played tackle. I came through the line with the ball and saw him standing there, staring up at the stars, not blocking anyone. I got behind him, put my hand on his back, and shoved him into an oncoming tackler. In the next huddle, he tried to apologize. I told him, "Just do your job." Of course, this was said loudly in front of the entire offensive unit of our football team.

During my senior year I managed to avoid contact with the guy. I never spoke to him again during the entire school year.

After graduation from high school, I went to college. Since I was now paying to go to class, I changed my ways and managed to get better grades in college than I had in high school. Like many in my college class, I got married and had kids. I began to attend high school reunions which were held every five years. I know some people hate reunions because some old classmates put on phony airs and lie about their accomplishments.

I admit almost all of my classmates were different. They didn't put on airs and spout nonsense about what they were doing. One common denominator of my class was they were from similar economic backgrounds, and they knew each other and generally liked and cared about each other. At one reunion I was sitting with a group of graduates when one girl in the group said she almost didn't come to the reunion. When asked why, she responded that life had not gone well for her, and she was not happy with where she was in her life. After a bit of silence, one of the guys in the group said, "We don't care about what's happened to you. We're just glad to see you." That remark pretty much summed up my class, and why I enjoyed our reunions.

When I went to the fortieth-class reunion, I was struck by the fact that my nemesis had never attended a single reunion when I was there. He sent letters to be read aloud to those in attendance. Most of them were almost laughable as excuses for not attending. One letter stated that he was in the cockpit of his airplane on the runway, but the fog was rolling in and he had to cancel the trip. What hogwash!

One of the more chilling moments at each reunion was when the names of classmates who had passed away since the last reunion were read. When you are eighteen, such a thing is unthinkable. When you are fifty-eight, it is sobering.

At each reunion I noticed changes in my classmates. For

most of the guys it was loss of hair and gain of weight. Some of the women had aged gracefully, but some had not.

Then I turned and found myself facing the same female classmate who had told several of us she almost didn't attend and why. After we shook hands, she looked at me and smiled.

"I want to thank you," she said.

"For what?" I replied with a puzzled look on my face.

"About two reunions ago, you were the host speaker. You talked about how much alike we all were and how much we had in common because of where we grew up and went to school. Then you told the story about the time I almost didn't come and what I blurted it out to the small group of classmates we were sitting with. You told the story well, but you were careful never to mention my name. When you got to the part where one of our classmates responded to me by saying, 'We don't care what happened to you. We're just glad to see you.' I remembered I never thanked you for not mentioning my name and embarrassing me."

I looked at her face and smiled. "Who you were wasn't the point. The point was we as a class and a group of friends cared about each other when we were growing up and we still feel the same way today."

She smiled back at me. Then we shook hands and separated to seek out more old classmates and to share old and new stories.

THE END

A STANGE CHRISTMAS

During the COVID epidemic, we found ourselves semi-voluntarily isolated in our home in the foothills west of Boulder, Colorado. Not a bad place to be isolated, but the lack of human contact had grown old, and it felt like going against the grain of our normal way of living.

It was December, and IU tried to think of other Christmas holidays in my past and wondered how strange this coming Christmas might be by comparison. Then I remembered the strangest Christmas Eve in my life. This is the story of that Christmas Eve.

In December of 1977, my family and I lived in Kemmerer, Wyoming. Kemmerer is a small town located about seven thousand feet above sea level. It sits in a small valley split by the Ham's Fork River. I had gone there to start a new National Bank charter in a town with only one bank that had been there since the town was founded.

One of the closer friends I made there was a sheep rancher named David Nelson. David was one of those people you meet who is actually larger than life. He was a small giant. He stood about six feet, four inches tall, with broad shoulders and the body of an NFL linebacker. He had huge hands and light blue eyes that seemed to twinkle when he was about to suggest some mischief. He truly was the man that John Wayne, the actor was supposed to be on the silver screen.

David and his wife Connie were two of the nicest people I had ever met. They had both sort of taken me under their wing and did they best to was the tenderfoot easterner out of me. David took me with him all over the county and as he showed me sites, he explained the history of the place, including who owned what land; how they got the land, and what happened to them. He was a walking local history book. In all my experiences with him, he was kind and thoughtful, in a rugged and no-nonsense kind of way. He treated me like a son, and I am forever indebted to him for his kindness and his attention. He taught me how to be a westerner. He taught me how to shoot and hunt. He taught me how to respect the land and how to survive in it, even during its harshest moments. I admired him then and still do today. I am thankful for every moment I got to spend with him. He gave me the equivalent of a post-graduate degree in dealing with life in Wyoming.

David and Connie had four children, two of whom, a son and a daughter, lived in Kemmerer. Both were married and had children. On Christmas Eve, David and Connie would visit their son and his family and then stop and visit their daughter and her family. Their daughter lived about two blocks from my house. After their visit to their daughter that Christmas eve, they came to our house and stopped in to see me and my family.

By about nine-thirty that Christmas eve, David and Connie left to go home, and my wife and I put our children to bed. Once the children were tucked in for the night, I returned to the living room to assume "Santa duties." I brought all the presents up from their hiding places in the basement and we put them around the Christmas tree. Then I tackled the assemble-by-steps projects. Finding tab A to put in slot B was always a challenge. I occasionally had to add a few choice cuss words to get some stubborn piece to finally lineup and slide together.

I had finished my assembly projects and was about to get ready for bed. It was almost midnight. Then the phone rang. I was surprised. No one ever called that late at night unless there was a serious problem. And it was Christmas Eve!

I went over and grabbed the phone. Connie was on the line. She said, "dave is coming to your house in the truck. He wants you out in front of your house and ready to go."

I was tempted to ask why, but I knew from experience and the tone in Connie's voice that any questions I had would be answered by David. I hung up the phone, grabbed my coat and gloves and rushed out the front door and then stood on the sidewalk. I didn't have to wait long.

David pulled up in his pickup truck and stopped a few feet from where I stood. I climbed into the passenger seat and clicked my safety belt on. When you rode with David, you took no chances.

David had changed clothes and was dressed in jeans and a flannel shirt with an old barn jacket. He wore no gloves. He waited until I clock my seat belt closed and then he put the truck in gear. We drove down the street. It was dark with no moonlight. There was no sign of anyone else out and about in a vehicle or on foot.

David drove two blocks down the street and then pulled the truck over and parked on the right side of the street. He left the engine running. I could see we were parked across the street from his daughter's house. I scanned thearea and could see no other vehicles or any signs of life.

After a few minutes of silence, I asked, "Why are we here?"

"My daughter's husband came home drunk again," said David. "He ignored her and the children and continued the drinking spree he had started at the bar over four hours ago."

I wanted to ask what that had to do with me, but I wisely kept my mouth shut and waited for David to continue.

"When she asked him to help her get the Christmas present out, he became enraged and he began to beat her," said David in a tone I had never heard from him before. It was a cold steel tone with a hard edge to it.

I waited for a few minutes, then I carefully asked him, "What are you planning to do?"

"We're gonna wait here and make sure she and her kids get their stuff out of the house and into her car without any interference from that drunken bastard," said David.

I thought about the situation and then I spoke again. "What happens if he comes out of the house and tries to stop her from leaving?"

David turned and looked over at me with the coldest blue eyes I have ever seen. He reached under the driver's seat and pulled out a pistol I recognized. It was his Colt Peacemaker single action forty-fi8ve caliber revolver. He laid the pistol on the seat between us. Then he looked over at me.

"If he tries to stop her from leaving, I'm gonna shoot and kill him", said David in a firm, but calm voice like he was ordering lunch at a restaurant.

I thought for a moment and then spoke. "Why am I here?" I asked.

"You're here as a witness I know I can count on," said David in a calm but hard voice.

"Oh, I said. I shut up and sat quietly in my seat as we watched his daughter and her two children exit the darkened house and finish loading up her car. Then they climbed into the car, and she drove off into the night. No one had come out of the house. The house was dark, quiet and motionless.

David waited until his daughter's vehicle's taillights disappeared and then he slid the Colt back under the driver's seat. He pulled away from the curb, did a U-turn, and drove back to the front of my house where he stopped.

I opened the passenger door and got out of his truck. Before I closed the door, David looked at me and said, "Thanks."

"You're welcome," I said and stood on the sidewalk, watching David drive away. Then I turned and went back to my house, trying to remember if I had forgotten any of my Christmas Eve chores to get ready for Christmas morning.

I couldn't think of any and went straight to bed. The next morning was a typical Christmas morning with the kids tearing open presents and having a wonderful time while my wife and I looked on.

David never mentioned the events of that night to me ever again. And I had the good sense to never bring them up.

THE END

THE COACH

I was reading local stories about coaches being fired and hired and it reminded me of this story.

I was watching the news on television one night about twenty-some years ago. The head basketball coach at Northwestern University in Evanston, Illinois, had just been fired by the school's athletic director.

Normally this was just more news. That night it was not. That coach was a friend of mine who had been a high school teammate. We grew up in a small town of about three thousand folks and went to a high school that had about two hundred and twenty students. You got to know everyone in the school. It was hard for me to imagine my friend being fired.

He was an excellent student and a great athlete. He was the quarterback of the football team, and he was the conference champion in the pole vault and the mile run on the track team. It was in basketball that he truly excelled. He led the state of Illinois in scoring and was placed on the Illinois All State basketball team along with four others from the Chicago area. Back then there was only one class of basketball team in Illinois and every school, large or small, was in it. My friend was good at everything he tried including both sports and academics.

He was recruited by schools like Kentucky, Louisville, Iowa, Purdue, and Illinois to play college basketball. He finally accepted a scholarship from Northwestern University. He told me he did so because he felt a degree from Northwestern would be a great asset to him in his later life. He started for Northwestern's team when he was only a freshman. He became a star player in the Big Ten Conference. He set a single game scoring record that still stands today. This was back before the three-point shot even existed. He scored forty-nine points against Iowa. He was selected to the Big Ten All-Conference team. He was an academic All American as well.

When he graduated with honors, the Boston Celtics drafted him. He declined the opportunity to play professional basketball and took a job as the freshman basketball coach at Northwestern University under coach Tex Winters. My friend stayed with the school as an assistant coach and when Tex Winters stepped down, my friend became the head basketball coach at Northwestern. He improved Northwestern's basketball team every year despite the handicap of the school's high academic standards that kept many good players from gaining admission. After several years he had his best team and took them to the National Invitational Tournament in Madison Square Garden in New York City. Then he had a few up and down years, and the result was the story I watched on television that night many years ago.

The next day I sat down and thought about my friend. All his life he had been a winner and someone who was exceptionally good at whatever he tried. I could only imagine how devastated he was feeling. I remembered how as a player in high school the level of his play on the basketball court made the rest of us look even better than we were.

I decided to sit down and write him a letter. In the letter I offered my support in what could not be a happy time for him. I told him that he had accomplished more in sports than anyone in the history of our small town. I reminded him of how he made everyone around him better by his style of play and his unselfish methods.

Then I repeated an old story. In one game in our home gym, I slipped past the boy guarding me and when one of our guys shot and missed, I had the inside position for a rebound on the weak side of the basket. I leaped up and grabbed the rebound. When I came down with the ball, I gave the guy guarding me a head fake. But instead of then going up with the ball to take a shot, I passed the ball out to the corner of the court where my friend was standing. He shot from the corner and made the basket.

A few minutes later we had a time out. My coach grabbed me by the arm in the huddle and asked me why I didn't take the ball back up when I was under the basket. My reply was that I thought about it but decided that my friend shooting from the outside corner was still better odds then me shooting from under the basket. The story was true, and I knew that my friend had used the story as a coach when he was trying to get his players to understand the importance of their individual roles on the team.

I finished my letter with telling my friend that no matter how dark things looked today, the sun was still coming up the next morning and, in this world, there is always a need for a good man.

I sent the letter and sure enough a week later I got a reply. My friend wrote and thanked me for forcing a little light into what had seemed like a very dark time to him and for reminding him of what a remarkable career he had enjoyed up until then.

A few years ago, I was watching the NCAA college basketball national championship tournament on television in March. During a break in the action, the television camera panned the crowd and then stopped on a well-dressed older man with a clipboard on his lap. The television announcers then identified him as my friend. They went on to comment that he was about to retire after over twenty years as the Assistant Commissioner in the Big Ten Conference in charge of basketball officiating, and what a wonderful job he had done for the Big Ten Conference and the game of college basketball.

I found myself smiling.

THE END

BRANDING TIME

I had traveled to Kemmerer, Wyoming, to start a new bank charter for a group of local investors. I arrived well ahead of my family and spent about five months in Kemmerer before they arrived. Housing was limited so I decided I was having a new house built on a lot in town I had purchased. During this time, I lived in a single wide trailer home out on a ranch belonging to the chairman of my investor group. There was one other building on the ranch, and it was an old bunkhouse. The sole occupant was a young Mexican sheepherder named Odie Lone.

There was no television reception and the only radio station I could find was KOMA in Oklahoma City. It disappeared from the airwaves promptly each evening at nine o'clock. Needless to say, there was little to do in the evenings and I began going to bed about nine in the evening.

I spent my days in a spare office in the chairman's place of business. I was on the phone to the Office of the Comptroller of the Currency each day for about four hours. The two-hour time difference between Wyoming and Washington, D.C., meant I started making phone calls about 7:00 A.M. each day and was shut down by 2:30 p.m. each day.

Every morning I drove into Kemmerer for coffee about

five o'clock. I met ranchers, both cattlemen and sheepmen, and various other businesspeople in town. I occasionally saw the chairman in the café, but not often. After about a month he came into my tiny office and told me he had a golden opportunity for me. A rancher who had purchased one of the chairman's old ranches was getting ready to brand his calves and needed manpower. The chairman had volunteered me. I should have noticed he didn't volunteer himself or either of his two fully grown sons. He said it would be a good opportunity to meet other cattlemen and establish myself in the community.

I had visions of me finally becoming a real cowboy, so I readily agreed. I should note that any resemblance between me and a real cowboy after a day of branding calves would be a grave mischaracterization.

I arrived at the ranch with one of the bank's investors, a younger man who worked as a foreman at the local coal mine. At approximately 5:45 A.M, real cowboys on horseback herded cows and calves into a makeshift corral set up on the corner of a large fenced-in pasture. The cowboys mounted their horses and soon separated the cows and calves, escorting the cows out of the corral and keeping the calves contained there.

Several other men, along with me and the coal foreman, were set up in teams of two. A mounted cowboy would rope a calf and drag him to an open area in the corral. Then he would halt his horse and keep the rope on the calf held tight. The foreman and I would follow the taut rope from the horseman to the calf. Then we would flip the calf on its side. The foreman would place his knee on the calf's shoulder, and I would take a seat at the rear of the calf where I would place a boot on the calf's butt. Then I would use my gloved hands to grab the calf's upper hind leg and pull it back towards me. This maneuver would render the calf basically immobilized.

Once the calf was in this position, other cowboys would vaccinate and dehorn the calf. Then a cowboy with a hot branding iron would press the iron on the calf's exposed rump, branding him with the ranch's brand. The hot branding iron on the hair and flesh of the calf smelled terrible to me and I'm sure the calf shared my sentiments.

The only thing different from this operation on this day to when it was done in the late 1800's was we used a propane fueled fire to heat the branding iron instead of a wood fire. Everything else was the same. The poor calves were terrified, and they usually emptied their bowels on the ground as they lay there helpless. Eventually, the coal foreman and I would either be sitting or kneeling in a mixture of mud, fresh calf dung and urine, blood, and sweat as we moved from one calf to another. At one point the coal foreman lost control of a calf and got kicked in the mouth. He was tough and didn't complain and kept on working as blood dripped from his mouth over the front of his shirt.

This went on continuously from 5:45 in the morning, until we were finished with the last calf at 2:30 in the afternoon. By the end of over nine straight hours of branding, my body was having trouble responding to my brain. At that point, a chuckwagon lunch was served to all the hands. I managed to stagger to my feet and get in the food line and get a plate of food. But when I went to sit down on the ground and enjoy my lunch, I found myself too exhausted to eat. I returned my plate, untouched, managed to say my goodbyes, and stiffly climbed into the front seat of my car. I drove to my little mobile home, parked the car, and struggled to get out of the front seat. When I got out of the car, my body was so stiff I could barely walk fifty feet to the front door of the trailer. I made it inside, went to the bathroom and put the plug in the bathtub drain and turned on the hot water tap. Then I staggered to the kitchen, shedding filthy, foul-smelling clothes as I went. I grabbed a cold six pack of Coors beer and returned slowly but surely to the bathroom, following the trail of clothing disaster. I wasn't sure if I should burn or bury my clothes. I managed to get into the tub now filled with hot water still gripping my cold liquid treasure and slipped into the hot soapy water. I stayed there for over three hours. When I finally emerged from the tub, the water was cold, and the last remaining can of beer was warm. I drank it anyway.

In the following months, I avoided all future opportunities to play cowboy. I was secretly thrilled I had survived my first real branding time, and it did earn me some respect from the locals. I also decided the reason there aren't many real cowboys left is they all got killed off trying to brand too many damn calves.

THE END

SAYING GOODBYE

My mother died just before her 93rd birthday. Shortly before her death she told me she never expected to live this long. I wasn't surprised that she did. She came from sturdy stock. Her father, a farmer, lived to be eighty-six. Her grandfather, who emigrated to the United States as a boy of twelve from Scotland, served in the Union Army under Sherman and survived four years of war without a scratch. He lived to be eighty-four.

As we drove from our home in Boulder, Colorado, to the tiny farm town of Galva, Illinois, the landscape and the weather reflected my feelings. The sun never appeared, the trees were bare of leaves and the sky was a dull metallic gray.

My wife Nancy was worried about how I was going to manage the task of saying goodbye forever to my mother. My wife is from the north shore of Chicago. She is a city girl, and she is used to what is often seen as an impersonal approach to others. This is somewhat typical of city dwellers. Even though our address is Boulder, Colorado, we live out in the country, which in Boulder means living on top of a foothill at an elevation of about eight thousand feet above sea level. We are close to the city, but we live in the country.

I was not with my mother when she passed away. She

had fallen and broken her hip. She was in a hospital in Galesburg, Illinois, and my two sisters were with her. It was on a Thursday when I was driving into Boulder when my cell phone rang. It was my sisters. They were with my mother, and they wanted me to tell her that it was all right to let go of her life.

"You want me to tell Mom it's all right to die?" I said with alarm in my voice.

They explained that Mom could not speak, but she could hear me and that they had already told her it was all right to let go. I had to think hard about it for a few minutes and finally I spoke on the phone and told my mother that it was all right to die. It was one of the hardest things I ever did in my life.

Two days later my brother-in-law called me and told me my mother had passed. I wept.

So now, we were back in my hometown of Galva, a small farming community in western Illinois, preparing to say goodbye to my mother for the last time.

In Galva, tradition calls for calling hours at the funeral home on the evening prior to the funeral. My wife was worried that I would be hurt and disappointed that few people would attend the calling hours or the funeral because my mother had outlived so many of her friends and relatives.

My mother had worked in Galva as an assistant librarian and then as a bank teller until she retired. In retirement she was active in her church and a Swedish social club among other groups. She also was part of a living history exhibit in nearby Bishop Hill State Park where she dressed in costume and used an antique spinning wheel made in Sweden to spin wool into yarn. Then she collected wild plants and used them to make dye to color the yarn. In her retirement my mother let no grass grow under her feet.

I assured my wife there would be enough folks who would stop by for the calling hours to pay their respects, even on a cold February evening in Illinois.

As part of the calling hours tradition, the family of the deceased stands in a receiving line and greets each person who has come to pay their respects. All of us were dressed in black, and my wife had on black high heels.

Galva is a small farm town of about two thousand eight hundred people. It is surrounded by farmland.

When all our family was properly set up in a receiving line, the funeral home operators opened the doors to initiate calling hours.

One by one, people came in a long steady line to pay their last respects and say goodbye to my mother. The line went on and on until two and a half hours had passed. I saw people I had not seen since I graduated from Galva High School in 1961. I met people that I had never known, but who knew of me because of my mother.

A little over twelve hundred people attended my mother's calling hours to say goodbye.

Afterwards my wife, her feet sore from standing so long in high heels, asked me how it was possible for so many to come to say goodbye.

I tried to explain how my family had been part of the area since my great grandfather returned from the Civil War to buy the family farm in 1873. I also knew that my mother had touched so many lives in the small town of Galva. The children whose savings accounts she had managed were now adults and they remembered her. It is also the tradition of small, midwestern towns to respect each other and is woven into the fabric of their everyday life and remains with you until the day you die.

I know my mother was not surprised by the turn-out for her calling hours or the funeral the next day. I believe she truly appreciated all of us for being there to say goodbye. I did.

THE END

THE LETTER

Sue tossed the small empty cardboard box into the corner of the room where she and her brother Al had piled each of their mother's "storage boxes" after carefully inspecting them for any contents.

"That's the last of them," she sighed.

"Thank God," replied her brother.

They were finally done going through their mother's attic where she had stored anything she considered valuable. Apparently "valuable" was loosely interpreted by their mother. Each piece of junk they found had to pass their mother's inspection before it could be discarded. Fortunately, most of the boxes turned out to be empty.

Their mother was moving into a retirement community condominium because she had finally grown weary of all the work associated with keeping up a house. Sue and her brother had flown back to Iowa for a long weekend to help their mother clean out her house. It was Sunday afternoon, and they were finally done.

They had just finished tossing all the empty boxes out of an attic window so they could collect them on the lawn below and were making their way to the narrow attic stairwell, when Al suddenly stopped and said, "What the heck is that?"

Sue looked up to where her brother was staring. Stuffed into a space above the stairwell frame was some kind of bundle. Al reached up and pulled the bundle loose from its hiding place. After he brushed off a heavy coat of dust, the bundle turned out to be a military duffel bag. Al carried the bag down the stairs, with Sue close behind.

They emerged into the hallway of the second floor of the old house and headed down the stairs to the kitchen where their mother was making a new pot of coffee. "Look what I found, Mom," said Al and he set the duffel bag down on the kitchen countertop.

Their mother's face seemed to drain of its color, and she slowly sat back down on the only remaining chair in the kitchen.

"What's wrong, Mom?" asked a concerned Sue.

Her mother paused, as if to catch her breath. After a few seconds of silence, she finally spoke. "Those are your father's personal effects from Vietnam. They send them to me after he was killed, and I never opened them. I put the bag in the attic and forgot about it."

"You never opened the bag to see what he left behind?" asked an incredulous Sue.

"It hurt me to even see the bag when they delivered it. Your father was dead, and nothing could replace him. All the bag did was remind me of how much I had lost. I put it away where it couldn't remind me of the hurt and the pain," she replied.

"Don't you want to see what's in it now?" asked Al.

"No. I didn't then, and I don't want to now," replied his mother.

"Can I have it?" asked Sue.

"If you promise to take it with you where I don't have to see it, that's fine with me," replied her mother.

Sue glanced at her brother. Al just shrugged his shoulders.

Their mother put her coffee cup down on the countertop and stood up. Then she walked out of the kitchen without another word.

Sue straightened out the duffel bag on the countertop and slowly pulled the zipper down the bag's length.

Carefully she began to remove the contents and place them on the countertop. There were folded uniform shirts and pants, a web belt, two olive drab caps, underwear, and socks. Then she removed a compact vinyl toilet kit stocked with a razor, soap, shaving cream, toothbrush, brush, and a small metal mirror. Near the bottom of the bag was a worn wallet containing her father's military ID and several cards. Next to the wallet were his dog tags on a simple chain.

"Is that all of it?" asked a curious Al.

"I think so," said Sue as she patted the bottom of the inside of the bag with her hand. "Wait, there's something else in here."

When she removed her hand, she was clutching a handful of photos and a brown manila envelope.

"Look. There's Dad," exclaimed Al as he held up one of the photos. The photo was of three soldiers standing arm in arm in front of a large tent. Their dad was the soldier in the middle of the trio. There were five photos and their father and one of the other two soldiers were in each photo. The men wore the worn fatigue uniforms of combat Marines. Stenciled over the pockets of their uniforms were their last names. It was easy to read the name "Collins" on the pictures of their father.

"Who is the other guy who is in all the pictures?" asked Al.

Sue squinted at the photo and said, "His name is Gunn."

"An appropriate name for a Marine," said Al. "What's in the envelope?"

Sue turned the envelope over and said, "It's a letter."

"A letter? Who's it addressed to?" asked Al.

"It's addressed to Mrs. Ruth Gunn, 216 Spruce Street, Boulder, Colorado," said Sue.

"Is that near where you live in Arvada?" asked Al.

"Actually, it is. How strange is that?" said Sue.

"So, who is she?" asked Al.

"Apparently she is married to the sender Roger Gunn," replied Sue.

"It must be the Gunn guy who is in the pictures with Dad," said Al.

"Why would this be in Dad's stuff?" asked Sue.

"I have no idea. Maybe he was supposed to mail it for the Gunn guy and never got to do it," suggested Al.

"Hard to believe it's been sitting in this bag for all these years. When did Dad get killed?" asked Sue.

"It was in 1968, in Hue. He was wounded and was being evacuated. The helicopter carrying Dad and other wounded Marines crashed just short of the hospital base. Dad and the others were all killed," said Al.

"I wonder what happened to the Gunn guy?" he said.

"I was thinking the same thing," said Sue as she tapped the envelope with her finger. "The return address shows

Roger Gunn. He must have written this to his wife and then given it to Dad to mail for him."

"So, we don't know if Mr. Gunn survived the war or even if his wife Ruth Gunn is still alive," said Al.

"One way to find out," said Sue. She left the kitchen and went outside to her rental car. She returned with her small laptop computer. She quickly plugged it in and attached a wireless module.

"Success," she said as the laptop booted up and she began tapping the computer's tiny keys.

"What are you doing?" asked Al.

"I'm using Google to check out Mr. Gunn. Umm. Not good," she said.

"What?" asked Al.

"Mr. Gunn was killed in the battle of Hue in 1968. He didn't make it out of Vietnam," said Sue.

"What about Mrs. Gunn?" asked Al.

"Checking on her now," said Sue as she punched out the proper keys.

"Hey. Mrs. Gunn is alive and well and still living on Spruce Street in Boulder," said Sue.

"After all this time that is amazing," said Al. "So, what do we do with the letter?"

"I think I'll take it home with me and drive up to Boulder and finish what our dad started by delivering the envelope in person," said Sue.

"Aren't you curious what's in the envelope?" asked Al.

"Of course I am, but this letter is for Mrs. Gunn, not us. The fact that this envelope has survived all this time tells me it was meant to be delivered to her," said Sue.

"You were always the incurable romantic, Sis. An

envelope that's been laying around all this time can't be all that important," said Al.

"Maybe and maybe not. If I were Mrs. Gunn, I'd want the chance to read what's inside the envelope," said Sue.

"For all you know they were getting a divorce and inside the envelope are the signed divorce papers," said Al.

"I could have done without the divorce reference, Al," retorted Sue.

"Oops. I'm sorry. I forgot you're still sensitive about your break-up with Jake. Three years should have been long enough to get over him," said Al.

Sue gave her brother a dirty look and unplugged her computer and packed it and the envelope in her computer case and took it out to her rental car.

A week later, Sue was home on a Friday night and decided to check out a web site on her laptop. As she pulled the laptop out of the case, the manila envelope slipped out and fell on the floor at her feet.

"Okay, okay, I'll deliver it tomorrow, "she said to herself.

Saturday morning and she placed the envelope in her purse and drove up the turnpike to Boulder. Sue drove through the town until she found Spruce Street and quickly found herself parked in front of a small light blue cottage with white shutters and a white front door centered on a small front porch.

She checked the address on the envelope, and it matched the number painted on the front of the small house. Before she got out of her car, she looked around. The yard was small and neat. Someone had planted bright colored flowers in large planters in front of the small porch. There was a driveway on the west side of the house which probably led to a garage behind the house. But something seemed out of place.

Parked in the driveway was a bright yellow Jeep Wrangler with a black top. Sue grinned as she tried to imagine her mother driving something like that. Maybe Mrs. Gunn was a lot livelier than Sue's mom. This was Boulder after all.

Sue got out of her car and walked to the front door. She paused on the front porch, located the doorbell, and pushed it. She waited and then she could hear footsteps in the house. The front door was pulled open, and she found herself face to face with a tall handsome man with jet black hair who looked to be about her age.

"Can I help you?" asked the man.

"My name is Sue Collins, and I think I have something that belongs to Mrs. Ruth Gunn," said Sue as carefully as she could manage.

"That would be my mother," said the man with a broad smile. "Please come in."

Sue entered the small but neat living room and the man motioned to an easy chair. "Please have a seat and I'll get my mother."

Sue took a seat on the antique easy chair and looked around the room. The furniture was old, but in good condition. The hardwood floor was covered with an attractive area rug. Sue looked up as the man returned with an old woman who bore a strong resemblance to the young man.

"Mother, this young lady is Sue Collins. Ms. Collins, this is my mother, Ruth Gunn. Pardon my lack of manners. I'm Roger Gunn, her son," he said.

"Roger Gunn?" said a surprised Sue.

"Actually, it's Roger Gunn, Jr. I was named after my dad," he said.

"How do you do, sue," said Mrs. Gunn in a pleasant voice, as she extended her hand and Sue responded by shaking it. "Please sit down," said Mrs. Gunn.

"Roger says you have something you think belongs to me. I don't recall losing anything." she said.

Sue paused and then spoke. "Actually, Mrs. Gunn, you didn't lose this. In fact, you never got it," said Sue.

Both Mrs. Gunn and Roger had puzzled looks on their faces. Sue went on to explain what happened during her trip back to Iowa to help her mother move.

When she finished, there was an awkward silence.

Mrs. Gunn broke the silence. "You found an envelope addressed to me sent to me by my husband? That hardly seems possible," said Mrs. Gunn.

"I assure you, Mrs. Gunn. I am not making this up. I found this envelope in my father's personal effects in his Marine duffel bag," said Sue.

"What did you say your last name was, dear?" asked a puzzled Mrs. Gunn.

"Collins, Sue Collins," replied Sue.

"Was your father a Marine named Todd Collins?" she asked.

"Yes," replied Sue.

"Oh my!" said Mrs. Gunn. She put her hand to her chest as if to reassure herself. She composed herself and then faced Sue.

"Was he killed in Vietnam?" she asked.

"Yes. He was killed in 1968 in a helicopter crash after he had been wounded in the battle of Hue," replied Sue.

Tears formed in Mrs. Gunn's eyes. She patted her chest with her hand until she composed herself. Then she looked up at Sue.

"My husband was killed in Hue in 1968. He had a close friend named Todd Collins that he often wrote about. They met in boot camp and went to Vietnam in the same company. I never knew what happened to Mr. Collins. How strange they would both die at the same time," she said.

Sue waited a moment and then she stood up and handed the envelope to a now weeping Mrs. Gunn. Roger stepped close to his mother and gave her a hug.

"I'm sorry, Miss Collins. Please forgive the foolishness of an old woman," said Mrs. Gunn.

"You have nothing to be sorry about, Mrs. Gunn. I feel the same way about my father. I never got to really know him," said Sue.

"Well, let's see what my dear Roger sent to us after all these years," said Mrs. Gunn. She slowly opened the envelope and pulled out a small white envelope with a folded sheet of paper.

"What's this?" said Mrs. Gunn. "It's an envelope with some writing on it and it is difficult for me to read it. Can you read it for me, dear?" said Mrs. Gunn as she handed the white envelope to Sue.

Sue turned the sheet of paper over and read aloud what she saw written there.

"To be read to my son Roger on the occasion of his first birthday.

I know it is hard for you to remember me, but I am your father. I cannot wait until I get home to you and your mother, and I look forward to doing all the things that fathers do with their sons.

I am not with you on your birthday because I am a Marine serving my country in a war in a foreign country called Vietnam. War is an ugly thing and I hope and pray you never have to experience the horrors I have witnessed here.

It is a hard thing to have to fight another person and know that you must kill them, or they will kill you. I fight for my country and to protect you and your mother. I fight to protect my fellow Marines and they fight for me. I pray that soon I will have to fight no more, and I can come home to you and your mother.

While I am gone, you are the man of the family and I look to you to take good care of your mother. Remember to always do what is right, even if it is hard. I will see you soon.

Happy Birthday, Son.

Love,
Your father
Roger Gunn
"Semper Fi"

Sue paused as she finished reading and looked up from the letter. Both Mrs. Gunn and her son were crying. Then she realized she was crying as well.

Later, when Roger walked her out to her car, he stopped, looked up at the foothills to the west, and then looked back at Sue.

"You did a wonderful thing today. You gave me and my mother a letter from heaven. You gave me a piece of my father that I never had. I will always be grateful to you for that. You also made my mother very happy," he said.

"All I did was deliver a letter," said Sue.

"You did a lot more than that. You did what your father would have done for my father. They were best friends for a reason. I think you and I could be best friends as well," said Roger.

"I'd like that," said Sue. Roger gave her a warm embracing hug.

As sue drove away, after exchanging contact information with Roger, she smiled.

"Thank you, Dad," she whispered.

THE END

CHRISTMAS LAWSUIT

Some parts of this story are actually true.

When I lived in Wyoming, I found many of the state's laws seemed a bit dated. Wyoming laws appeared to be forty years behind the rest of the country. I found that somewhat comforting.

I lived in Kemmerer, Wyoming, which is in Lincoln County. Lincoln County was not an original county and was added after Wyoming statehood was granted. It was carved out of neighboring counties. The north half of Lincoln County was heavily settled by Mormons and was largely agricultural. The southern half of the county was also agricultural, but had added coal mines, coke mines, and an electric power plant fueled by the nearby supply of coal.

Late one year a court case evolved that raised my curiosity. Because of the two main characters involved and the issue at hand, I found myself faking an excuse to slip away from my job at Fossil Butte National Bank and sliding into a back seat in the county courthouse. Kemmerer was and is the county seat of Lincoln County.

The main characters on stage in the courthouse were the judge, the plaintiff, and the defendant. The presiding judge was Judge Christmas. No, that's not a spelling error. That was the judge's last name. The plaintiff was the president of the other bank in Kemmerer. The defendant was a heavy equipment contractor.

The case was a suit for partition of a piece of real estate the two parties owned jointly as tenants in common. Tenants in common means each party owned an undivided half interest in the real estate. The purpose of such a suit is to split the property into two separate parcels with each party owning one hundred percent of their individual parcel. The result was splitting the land between the two joint owners.

The reason for the suit was the contractor had fallen on hard times, and the banker partner was afraid of lawsuits filed by unpaid creditors of the contractor that might encumber the banker's interest in the real estate.

The contractor had purchased an old two-story brick house down by the Ham's Fork River. The house, known as the Southern Hotel, had enjoyed a previous fifty- year history as a house of ill repute. About five years before, a Mormon from the north end of Lincoln County had been elected county sheriff. He had seen fit to close the slightly illicit, but highly popular and profitable entertainment business. The fallout was a lot of muted outrage, but the Southern Hotel remained closed until it was purchased by the contractor for his residence. The contractor had five daughters and on more than one occasion, nighttime visitors appeared at the front door of the old building looking for female companionship. The result was often confusion, anger, and hilarity.

Once the court was called to order, things moved quickly. A large map of the disputed real estate parcel was set up on an easel. The attorney for the banker pointed out the real estate was about two hundred acres of mostly rolling hills populated only by clumps of sagebrush, but that the land bordered a portion of the Ham's Fork River. Near the river, about twenty-five acres of the two hundred acres contained a large gravel deposit. It was the only valuable portion of the entire real estate parcel.

Judge Christmas listened intently as the attorneys for both the plaintiff banker and the contractor defendant made their client's case and vigorously attempted to answer each of the judge's questions.

Finally, the judge tired of the proceeding and the yammering of the two attorneys. He directed the attorneys to return to their seats and called for the banker and the contractor to come forward and approach the bench. The judge then ordered both parties to face the easel with the map on it. The judge called the bailiff to his podium and handed the bailiff a magic marker.

The judge looked down on the banker and the contractor. He stared at them for a moment and then he spoke.

"I will grant the request for partition of the land in question, but with two conditions," he said.

Both the banker and the contractor leaned forward, eager to hear the conditions.

"One of you will take this magic marker and then use it to divide the real estate parcel on the map into two separate parcels. When he is finished, the other one of you will get first pick of the now established parcels," said the judge with a grim smile on his face.

Both men were stunned into silence.

"Merry Christmas," said the judge as his stern face broke into a huge grin. "Who wants to go first?"

The bailiff stood next to the map, holding out the magic marker in his outstretched hand.

Justice was served. Just in time for Christmas.

THE END

THE BLACK FOREST CAKE

This is a true story. Well, some of it is true.

When my wife Nancy and I were first married, we lived in an apartment in Bourbonnais, Illinois. We were about to celebrate my first birthday as Nancy's husband, and she wanted it to be special. She invited her parents to travel down from Zion, Illinois, for a special dinner. She is a meticulous planner in everything she does. As she was making her grocery list for the planned dinner, she asked me what kind of birthday cake I wanted.

I am actually a pie guy. I have no idea how the custom started, but all throughout my childhood, I had pie for my birthday. Strawberry-rhubarb is my favorite pie. I mentioned a pie, but she scoffed at the idea and said a birthday party demands a cake.

I thought about it and remembered seeing a special kind of cake in a bakery in town. Then I remembered the name. It was a Black Forest Cake. It had looked terrific in the display case at the bakery. So, I blurted out I would like a Black Forest Cake.

I should have known better.

Nancy grabbed her cookbook, found the cake section, and started making a list of ingredients she would need. My birthday was the next day, so she went to the store to obtain all the required items she did not have in her kitchen. When she returned from the grocery store, she unloaded all the items from bags onto the kitchen counter.

She put on a fancy apron and began to measure and sort all the ingredients and put them into a large mixing bowl. A Black Forest Cake, she explained, is a moist chocolate sponge cake in two layers with homemade whipped cream frosting and fresh cherries. Then she snapped her fingers as she remembered something.

She was short of one ingredient for the recipe. The ingredient was Luxardo Cherry Liqueur. I had never heard of it. She directed me to go to the liquor store and buy a bottle, while she began putting the ingredients for the cake together.

I dashed out to my car and drove to the local liquor store. When I asked for Luxardo Cherry Liqueur, the clerk looked at me like I was speaking Chinese. Then he told me he didn't have any, had never had any, and didn't plan to have any, ever.

I thanked the clerk and went back to my car and drove to another liquor store. No dice. I went to four liquor stores and came up empty. No one had Luxardo Cherry Liqueur.

I got lucky at the last store. The clerk suggested I try a liquor store in the Black neighborhood of the neighboring city of Kankakee. This was an area known as the North Side. I followed his directions, found the store, and parked my car and went inside. The store was small, dark, and empty of any clientele. I explained to the clerk what I wanted. She scratched her ear, and then her eyes lit up. She slipped into a small back room and came out with a bottle of Luxardo Cherry Liqueur. The bottle was white, but it was encrusted with years of dust and grime. It was more grey than white.

I paid for the bottle and rushed back to the apartment. I proudly presented the bottle to Nancy. She thanked me and then cleaned off the bottle and placed it next to her cake ingredients.

Having done my husbandly duty, I retreated to the living room and the safety of the television set.

After a while I heard a ding from the timer in the kitchen. I looked up and saw Nancy leaning down in front of the oven. She had cooking mittens on both hands. She opened the oven door and then carefully took out the first layer of the cake and set it on top of the counter. Then she bent down for a second time and began to pull out the second layer of the cake. Something went wrong.

As she was removing the second layer of the cake from the oven, the layer slipped off the baking pan and fell down inside the oven. Half of it fell into the oven and half of it fell out on the top of the open oven door. The cake was ruined.

Nancy tried to rescue the portion of the cake that landed on the oven door with a spatula. The half cake slid off the spatula and fell down on the open oven door where it suffered more significant cake injuries. Nancy knelt by the open oven and stared at the broken cake in absolute shock. Then she used the spatula and attempted to rescue the now broken half cake. The effort failed and pieces of cake dropped onto the open oven door.

Then my wife lost her temper. She took the spatula and began to pick up pieces of the broken cake. She started flinging pieces over her shoulder, over her head, behind her and to the side of her. Cake flew in all directions. I have never seen a spatula move that fast nor see more cake airborne at one time.

Finally, she ran out of cake and sat down on the kitchen floor in defeat. She got up, cleaned herself off, and began making another cake. I wisely made an excuse to vacate the premises, telling my wife I needed to get the car washed. When I returned, she had made a second cake, and it was perfect.

The next day, my birthday dinner with her parents was a complete success. The dinner was perfect and so was the cake. One would never know the same kitchen the day before had been the scene of a culinary disaster.

Pieces of that cake appeared in all sorts of weird places in the kitchen for the next four months.

THE END

MY FIRST PICKUP TRUCK

In 1975, I took a job starting up a new national bank charter in the small town of Kemmerer, Wyoming.

Since the time difference between Washington, D.C., and Kemmerer was two hours, this led to some strange delays in getting answers from the folks at the folks at the office of the Comptroller of the Currency in Washington, D.C.

Every morning, I would meet with my boss, the chairman of the bank, at a café for coffee at 5:00 A.M. In one of our first meetings, he asked me if I owned a pickup truck. I told him no; I had never owned a pickup truck.

He informed me I was going to need one living in Kemmerer. I asked him why. He said, "What will you do if your washing machine goes out?"

"I'll call the repairman," I said.

"The nearest repairman is in Salt Lake City, almost three hours away," he replied. "You need a pickup truck to take it to the repair shop. Same goes for almost everything else you own."

Two days later he arrived for coffee and told me had had found me a pickup truck. After coffee we drove out to a nearby ranch. The rancher had died two years before, and his pickup truck was still parked next to a shed on the ranch.

I eased out of his Jeep Wagoneer and stared at this

potential purchase. The truck was a 1949 GMC ¾ ton pickup truck with a removable stock rack. It had once been painted some shade of green, but now there was more bare metal showing than faded green paint.

Nonetheless, I bought the truck from the rancher's widow for the surprising sum of $50. We towed it to Kemmerer to a repair shop. On the advice of the mechanic, I added new tires, new distributor cap, new spark plugs, wiring, and a new battery.

When he was done with the truck, I paid him the princely sum of $450 and got in the cab. It started immediately and the old six-cylinder motor ran smoothly. I was hooked.

I drove that old truck everywhere. I kept saying it was going to take the stock rack off, but I never did. I loved that old truck, even the rusty stock rack. I drove it everywhere, including my exploratory trips to the nearby hills and mountains.

Winter came and the old GMC went through snow like it wasn't there. I drove it to Salt Lake City several times and it never failed me. In really cold weather it always started. One morning it was twenty-five degrees below zero, and the old GMC fired up immediately.

On the day before we were to open the bank officially for business, I went over our check list with my Cashier. Everything was fine until I got to the item, "Cash."

My Cashier told me she had ordered $700,000 in cash from the Federal Reserve Bank in Dener, but it had not arrived. I told her to call the Fed. She did and then told me they had mailed it to us.

"Mailed it to us," I said incredulously. "You mean like to our Post Office Box here in Kemmerer?"

She nodded her head to indicate yes, and we called the post office in Kemmerer. They informed us they had the shipment from the Federal Reserve Bank in Denver and when were we coming to pick it up?

I was sort of stunned as I made my way to our parking lot. I got in the old GMC and drove up the hill to the post office. I went inside and up to the counter and identified myself and my purpose. They asked if I had a pickup truck. I told them yes and was informed I should drive to the rear of the post office building to the loading dock.

I drove the old GMC around the building to the rear and backed up to their loading dock. I had barely shut off the engine when three men came out and opened the back of the stock rack on the old truck. They then began tossing sacks into the bed of the old GMC. When they were done, one of them came up to me so I could sign a receipt for the shipment. I signed and he gave me a copy and disappeared back into the post office building.

I climbed back into the cab of the old GMC. I started the engine and pulled out of the parking lot. As I drove down the hill to the site of my new bank, I smiled to myself.

I was driving to the bank in broad daylight in a 1949 GMC ¾ ton pickup truck with a faded paint job and an old rusty stock rack with seven hundred thousand dollars in currency and coins in the bed of the truck. Who would believe it? Certainly not any of the good citizens of Kemmerer. Most certainly not any bank robbers and thieves. The entire notion was too goofy and dumb to be real.

I laughed all the way down the hill to the bank.

THE END

THE POLITICIAN

When I moved to Kemmerer, Wyoming, from Illinois in 1976, it was a combination of culture shock and as if I had fallen into a time warp and ended up in a place much different than I was prepared for.

I was from a small farming town, Galva, Illinois, and had worked on our family farm in Altona, Illinois. The family farm produced corn and soybeans and raised hogs. To save money and avoid expensive fertilizers, we rotated crops and moved the hog operations from field to field each year. When commodity prices were low, the farm bought cattle from western herds and fed them on our feedlot to then sell them in Chicago as fat cattle.

I thought I knew a bit about agriculture as a business. I was wrong.

I learned about raising sheep and cow-calf operations and bailing wild hay. Wyoming was like a different world to an Illinois country boy.

I was fortunate to make good friends of several ranchers and one of them took the time and trouble to take me under his wing and teach me about an entirely different world of agriculture.

Wyoming is a huge state and has only a small number of people living there. The two largest cities, Casper, and Cheyenne, each only hold about fifty thousand people. To say you know almost everyone in the state is not much of an exaggeration.

I should start with the premise that the laws in Wyoming are probably forty to fifty years behind the laws in most states. And folks in Wyoming like it that way.

It was a hot July Sunday. David Nelson, one of the two biggest sheep ranchers in the state, had befriended me. I'm not sure why. I know he saw me as a complete greenhorn. He went out of his way to teach me about sheep, cattle, and the history of the Ham's Fork Drainage.

On this Sunday he pulled up to my house in his GMC four-wheel drive pickup truck and asked if I'd like to go for a ride. I was happy to oblige him. Every outing with David Nelson had been like an education course for me. This time we drove out to his ranch and checked on some heifers he had just purchased. We checked on the cattle, tossed them several bales of hay, and made our way back to Kemmerer.

Unlike many towns, Kemmerer downtown is built around a triangle park, not a square. Back then every other building on the Triangle was a bar. At the bottom of the social scale of bars was the Star Bar. It was so bad the bar's softball team called themselves the Star Bar Trash and wore t-shirts to prove it. At the other end of the scale was the Stock Exchange Bar. David parked the truck and we walked into the Stock Exchange Bar, found an empty booth, and ordered two beers. The bar was deserted except for the two of us and the bartender.

After about ten minutes of drinking and chatting, the

door to the bar swung open and in walked two men. They looked alike but were dressed very differently. One of them was dressed like David and me, but the other was dressed in a well-pressed, clean jump suit. He looked as out of place as a thief in church.

The two newcomers grabbed beers at the bar and joined us in our booth. The cowboy of the two was the other big sheep rancher in Lincoln County. He introduced the other man as his visiting brother.

It turned out his brother had just returned from Iraq where he was the United States Assistant Ambassador and had worked closely with the then ruling Shah of Iran. I asked him what he was doing now, and he replied he was "indisposed."

I took that to mean he was between political jobs.

We four drank and chatted some more. About twenty minutes later the door to the bar swung open again and in walked a tall, lanky cowboy dressed in denim, and wearing a battered brown cowboy hat. He took off the hat and used it to smack his shirt and pants to knock the dust off. He ordered a beer and then brought it to our booth.

We shook hands and he introduced himself as Ed Herschler, Kemmerer cattle rancher and the current Governor of the State of Wyoming.

So, there I sat in a booth in a bar in Kemmerer, Wyoming with the two largest sheep ranchers in the state, a former United States Assistant Ambassador to Iran, and the governor of the State of Wyoming.

We sat back and chatted for a bit. I sat there, keeping my mouth shut, with a huge smile on my face.

Finally, David Nelson looked over at me and asked me if I was all right. He said I looked a bit strange.

I looked at the group around me and said, "This could never happen in Illinois."

And it couldn't.

THE END

THE FENCE

This summer a longtime friend of mine passed away at the age of eighty-nine. David Nelson was one of those people who you occasionally run into who are larger than life. He stood six foot four inches tall, and he weighed about two hundred and fifty pounds. He had broad shoulders, large hands, and bright- blue eyes. He looked every bit like the Vikings who were his ancestors.

He was born on a homestead on the Hamm's Fork River and near the tiny town of Opal, near Kemmerer, Wyoming. He spent most of his life running sheep in the Hamm's Fork Drainage.

I met him when I moved to Kemmerer in 1975. He then owned one of the two biggest sheep operations in Wyoming. He took a liking to me and treated me like I was part of his family. Most of what I know of western life and culture I learned from him. He was a man who came close to what you would expect from John Wayne. He lived a life that was full of hard work, nasty weather, and considerable dangers. He was as tough as the land he worked. Although he could be an intimidating force, he had a soft and gentle side to him when it came to people in need.

This is a story of what would be typical for him when it

came to helping others and the kind of help you might expect when you lived in a small town in Wyoming.

I had decided to build a red cedar wooden fence around the backyard of my house in Kemmerer. To do so I had to first buy the fencing material. That required two trips to Sutherland's Lumber in Salt Lake City, a hundred and thirty-five miles away in my three-quarter ton Ford pickup truck pulling a utility trailer. After unloading all the fencing material, I decided I would start work on the fence on Saturday afternoon when I got home from work at the bank.

I set posts in the ground at each corner and then ran string from post to post. Then I measured the proper distance for the location of each post hole and put loose chalk on the ground to mark the spots for each post. Then I brought out my two-handed post hole digger and began to dig the first hole. The ground was rocky and just getting one hole dug was a chore.

I had just finished digging the first post hole when one of my bank customers came by in his pickup truck. He stopped to observe what I was doing. Then he looked at my newly dug hole and said, "I'll be right back."

Fifteen minutes later he was back on a tractor with a post-hole digger attached to it. In half an hour he quickly and efficiently dug all my marked post holes. I thanked him profusely and offered to pay him, but he would take nothing. We shook hands and he left on his tractor.

Then I began to wrestle the first of many fence posts into the first post hole. I had no sooner gotten the fence post into the hole when David Nelson drove up in his pickup. He got out and looked over my backyard with the fencing material and the newly dug post holes.

"Are you using concrete in the bottom of the post holes?" he asked.

"Concrete?" I said in a bewildered voice.

"Come with me," he said, and we drove down to his warehouse in the neighboring village of Diamondville. He opened the large entry door to the warehouse and stepped inside and switched on a light.

There on one side of the old warehouse was a huge pile of sacks of concrete on pallets. There must have been five hundred sacks of the stuff. David explained that he often bought things like concrete as salvage from semi-tractor trailed wrecks, which occurred quite often in Wyoming, especially in the winter.

David looked at me. "Don't just stand there. Let's get this stuff loaded," he said.

We quickly loaded up his pickup truck with about fifty bags of concrete and then returned to my house. With David directing and helping, we set all the fence posts in a base of fresh concrete and then filled in the holes with dirt and tamped the dirt flat. By the time we were done it was dusk.

I brought out two beers from my house and we sat on the ground and drank them. When we had finished, David got up to leave. I asked him what I owed him, and he just gave me a smile, winked at me, and said, "Merry Christmas."

I have used David Nelson as the model for one of the main characters in my novels and I will continue to do so. It is my way of thanking him and keeping him alive in my memory.

I miss him.

THE END

THE WRAPPING PAPER

I grew up in a one parent family, my father having died when I was eight years old. I got my first job when I was twelve as a delivery boy for the Rock Island Argus newspaper. The Argus wasn't really that popular in my small hometown of Galva, Illinois, and I was hired as a delivery boy for the Galesburg Register Mail after just six months. This was a great job as the paper was very popular and my paper route covered about a fourth of the town.

By the time I went to college, I had worked at many jobs ranging from working on my uncle's farm to working on a crew removing dead elm trees for the city. The Dutch Elm disease had killed many of the majestic elms that lined one of the main thoroughfares of Galva. My mother had remarried when I was sixteen and I acquired two stepsisters as part of the deal. Both were older and married. I also acquired a step-brother-in-law who had built a career as a car salesman. When my stepsister became pregnant, my step brother-in-law Johnny decided to change professions.

Johnny was a born salesman. He had risen to general sales manager of the Ford, Lincoln, and Mercury dealer in nearby Kewanee. He quit his job and bought a small men's clothing store in Galva from two elderly brothers who wanted to retire. Their store was old, tired, and not very busy. Johnny quickly changed that. He had big sales to get rid of old merchandise and then cleaned up the store and restocked it with fresh new merchandise. Business quickly picked up and the store became remarkably busy.

I started working for Johnny on a part-time basis in high school. I worked as a salesclerk on Saturday evenings. I also worked at a local gas station on Thursday nights, Saturdays, and every other Sunday. On Saturday I would rush home after working at the gas station, take a bath, change clothes, and hurry down to the store. In addition to being an excellent salesman, Johnny was a good teacher.

He made sure I understood the following rules when I was working in the store. Always greet the customers when they enter the store. Then ask them if you can help them. Most customers want to look around and dislike being pressured by salespeople. They will usually reply that they are just looking. To offset this, the rule was to tell them to let you know if they had any questions and then work restacking merchandise while keeping an eye on them. As soon as you saw them gaze around with a puzzled look on their face, you moved near them, and they almost always had a question.

Another rule was to make sure the customer made the final decision. A woman might come in near Christmas and be looking for a pair of pajamas for her husband. You would spread out the assorted styles and colors of pajamas on the countertop for her to inspect. If she became frustrated and said, "I can't decide which one to pick. You're a man. Which one would you choose?" I would respond by selecting two pairs of pajamas and tell her I thought either one of them would be an excellent choice. Thus, she ended up making the final decision and how her husband felt about the pajamas were on her and not the salesclerk or the store.

A final rule was when the customer brought their purchases to the counter to pay for them, you would always say to them, "Will there be anything else?" It was amazing to me how many people would then say, "Do you have this, or do you have that in stock?" Johnny's theory was they were already there in the store and if they had something else in mind, why make another trip.

Galva is a small farm town and a store like Johnny's is likely to sell more bib-overalls than suits. Suits were largely for church, weddings and funerals, and graduations. As discretionary income grew, the store sold a lot of clothes to you men. Johnny once had a visit from the president of the HIS Clothing Company who at that time made a popular brand of men's pants. He came to see the store that had sold more pairs of HIS pants in the past year than there were people in the town.

The store was open from 9 a.m. to 5 p.m. from Monday through Saturday. It was also open to 8 p.m. on Friday and Saturday nights when the farm families came to town to shop. The exception to the rule was Christmas Eve. The store stayed open until 9 p.m. on that one night of the year.

I was home from college for Christmas break during my freshman year. As soon as I got home, I started working full-time at the store for Johnny. It was the week before Christmas, and he needed all the help he could get. We were so busy we rarely closed the store at 5 p.m. We didn't close until all the customers were served and had left the store. That was usually around 6 p.m.

You didn't just help shoppers find what they wanted and

then ring up the sale. You also had to wrap all the purchases for them. We had boxes I various shapes and sizes and you had to put them together. We had a huge roll of Christmas wrapping paper on a stand that let you pull out the paper to the size you needed and then lifted the paper where an attached blade cut the paper to the required size.

Christmas Eve fell on a Saturday that year. I thought the heavy shopping traffic would fall off by around 5 p.m., but it didn't. We were busy up through about 8 p.m. By then it had started to snow outside, and the shoppers began to dwindle in number. At about 8:30 p.m. the store was finally empty.

We all sort of breathed a sigh of relief and I noticed that Johnny was looking at his watch. Five minutes later the little bell on the front door rang, and the door opened, and a shopper entered the store. We all looked up and here was this very small, elderly lady. She was dressed in an old worn coat that had seen better days but was still clean and neat.

I started to approach the lady, but Johnny motioned for me to stay put. He went forward and asked her if she needed any help and she said she was just looking. She then spent about ten minutes wandering around the aisles in the store and finally she came to the counter with a small box of white handkerchiefs in her hand. It was probably the cheapest item we had in the store.

As Johnny rang up the sale, the lady began to speak. She told Johnny that he had the most beautiful Christmas wrapping paper she had ever seen. She went on to say how colorful it was and what a high quality of paper it was. This went on for several minutes. Johnny went over to the wrapping counter and cut off a small amount of it to wrap the elderly lady's small purchase. When he was finished, he then pulled off several yards of the wrapping paper and rolled it into a tube. He fastened the loose end to the tube with scotch tape and handed it to the lady.

"Merry Christmas, ma'am, and thanks for your business," said Johnny with a smile.

When the elderly lady had left the store, Johnny locked the front door after her and turned to look at the rest of us. "Every Christmas Eve, that old lady shows up just before closing time and makes a small purchase and then compliments me on my wrapping paper. This has been going on for five years and has become a Christmas tradition for me. I will be extremely disappointed when Christmas Eve comes and she doesn't' come in the store," said Johnny.

I worked for Johnny on Christmas Eve for the next three years and she showed up for every one of them.

THE END

THE WEDDING

This is a true story. Well, some of it is.

My wife Diana and I had hosted the rehearsal dinner in a restored old mansion in Grand Rapids, Michigan, which had been converted into a loverly restaurant. During the dinner, I could tell my son Tom, the groom, was worried and I was painfully aware of the source of his concern. Tom, my mother, my wife, and I made up the entire wedding party for the groom.

He and his future bride, Shannon, a lovely girl, had decided to get married in her hometown of Grand Rapids, Michigan, during the Christmas season. Everything had been carefully planned and accounted for and we were there on the evening of the wedding. The ceremony was to take place in her family's small church and then the reception was to be held at one of the larger hotels in the city. The only cloud on the horizon for most folks was the possible threat of a snowstorm on the day of the wedding.

Tom's concern had nothing to do with the weather. His mother and I had been divorced for over a dozen years, and the divorce had been bitter and contentious. So bitter, in fact, that his mother had told each of our three children that if they ever married and had the nerve to invite their father, she would not attend. Not only would she not attend, but no one on her side of the family would attend, nor any of their friends.

While Tom had shared his concern with Shannon, it was obvious that neither she nor her family took the threat of Tom's mother boycotting the wedding seriously. What mother would not want to be there when one of her children was getting married?

I knew Tom was probably right about his mother. He had told me he was sure he was going to be embarrassed when the tables at the reception reserved for his family would be empty except for me, my wife, and my elderly mother. Three people would hardly fill up an area reserved for twenty.

The church service was restricted to immediate family and a few guests as the chapel was very small and seating was extremely limited. The church was already decorated for the Christmas season. Tom wasn't worried about the wedding service. He was concerned about the reception.

I did have an ace in the hole. My older sister, Mary, lived in a suburb of Detroit and her children, all five of them, either lived in Michigan or were visiting her for the holidays. All of them had been invited to the reception. Still, with the weather threatening a snowstorm it was possible they might not be able to make it to the wedding reception.

The wedding day arrived cloudy, grey, and cold. After all, it was winter in the Midwest. I grew up in the Midwest and my memories of winter for all those years consisted of the sun never shining, my feet were always cold, and the snow got yellow in December and stayed that way until spring.

The wedding went off perfectly. The bride was lovely, and the groom looked nervous, but handsome. My wife squeezed my hand as the bride and groom exchanged their vows and we smiled at each other. I had carefully scanned the church for any sign of my ex or her family. I saw no one I knew except for my wife and my mother.

After the newly married couple made their escape from the church, I gathered up my wife and mother and drove to the hotel. We made our way to the ballroom where the reception was to be held. It was lovely and decorated with white bells, angels, and flowers. There were two bars, and I promptly made my way to the nearest one and ordered the first adult beverage I could think of. Once I had my drink in hand, I leaned back against the bar and carefully scanned around the room. The ballroom was rapidly filing up and people were taking seats at the tables. Just as Tom had feared, the group of tables reserved for his family looked quite deserted.

After a while, the wedding party arrived, and Tom and Shannon came by to say hello and accept our congratulations. Both my wife and my mother seemed very pleased. I found myself watching the main door of the ballroom, hoping for the cavalry or something like that, to arrive. I had noticed my son Tom had looked sadly at the empty tables surrounding the three of us while he was talking to my wife and my mother.

Finally, the announcement came for everyone to be seated and the waiters began serving the dinner they had prepared for the wedding party. After serving the rest of the guests, the waiters finally made their way to the island of empty tables next to our little party of three. The waiters were just placing our plates in front of us when the double doors to the ballroom burst open. In trooped my sister, Mary, all five of her children, their spouses and all their children. They numbered about twenty. They still had snowflakes clinging to their coats and hats and their cheeks were red from the cold. They looked like a scene out of an old Christmas movie minus Jimmy Stewart.

Very quickly our island of empty tables became a sea of voices and laughter as our late arrivals shed their coats and hats and made themselves at home. After the meal they all mingled well with Shannon's family and guests. When the band began playing, they literally took over the dance floor and spread their infectious feelings of joy and having a good time throughout the entire room.

I took a moment to check out my son Tom at the head table and his face was beaming. His fears were gone. His family had arrived.

I have never told my sister Mary how important it was for her and her family to be at Tom's wedding, but in one fell swoop she and her children and grandchildren wiped out any sense of dread that existed and replaced it with pure joy and love.

Family is one of the greatest assets you can ever have. Especially during the Christmas season and especially when they show up just in time.

THE END

STEWED TOMATOES

Growing up, we didn't have much money, but we never went hungry. One of the reasons was my mother always had a sizeable vegetable garden. One of the most productive plants in her garden was the tomato plant. She canned stewed tomatoes by the bucket load. The downside was that in the fall and winter, we ate stewed tomatoes at least three times a week.

I wasn't a fussy eater, but I grew to hate stewed tomatoes. When I finally left home to go off to college, I vowed I had eaten my last mouthful of stewed tomatoes. That lasted until 1979, eighteen years after I left home for college.

I was living in Kemmerer, Wyoming, and was part of a hunting group headed up by Big Dave Nelson. WE had about ten men in our hunting party. We drove pickup trucks and towed horse trailers and camping trailers to a trailhead at the base of Commissary Ridge. It was located west of the small town of LaBarge, Wyoming. There we set up our base camp including a corral for the horses.

On opening day, we saddled up our horses and headed up a narrow path on the face of the ridge that led all the way to the top for one thousand feet. Commissary Ridge reached a height of about ten thousand feet above sea level. The top of the ridge was flat for about two hundred feet from one side to the other. The east side of the ridge was sheer. The west side of the ridge tapered down through various gullies and washes.

We set up camp on top of the ridge with two tents. One was a larger Baker wall tent and the other a smaller umbrella tent. The Baker tent had a small wood stove we could use for cooking and heating. We were up early on opening day and had a quick breakfast and then split up into small groups to set up ambushes at the head of the various gullies and washes on the west side of the ridge. About an hour after the sun came up, we heard two shots from several gullies to the north of us. We knew this was part of our group, so somebody had been lucky enough to have elk choose to enter their ambush site.

About an hour later it started to snow. Not just snow, but snow with flakes the size of silver dollars. It began to snow hard. We abandoned our ambush site and struck out for the location where we had heard the gunfire. When we got there, one of our hunting party had indeed shot a large bull elk.

They pulled the bull elk up the hill to a level spot and began to field dress it. I and one other hunter were chosen to head back to camp to start a fire in the stove and get it ready to make supper while the rest of the party prepared the carcass for transport.

The two of us headed up the side of the ride to reach the top. The snow was coming down hard and I could barely see two feet in front of me. We reached the top and then turned right to head to our tents. In the snowstorm we got disoriented and suddenly found ourselves on the edge of the top of the ride, looking down one thousand feet in the whirling snow. We carefully turned to our right and followed the edge of the ridge until we could see the outline of one of the tents. We reached the tents and started a fire in the stove. Both of us were relieved to be out of the snow and cold. We checked on the horses and brought in more firewood. By the time the rest of the crew arrived with the elk meat, the fire was hot, and the big tent was warm.

Big Dave made supper and when I went up to have my tin plate filled with hot food, a substantial portion of our meal was stewed tomatoes. In the interest of survival and hot food, I ate all of it and went back for seconds. Stewed tomatoes never tasted so good.

That night the snowstorm continued, and we got a total of slightly over two feet. About three in the morning, the umbrella tent collapsed under the weight of the snow and the occupants were forced to move over to the Baker tent until morning.

We were up at sunrise. We skipped breakfast, broke down and packed our gear, and saddled our horses. We led, not rode, our horses down the snow-covered narrow trail on the face of the east side of the ridge to our base camp. Once there we unloaded the horses and put them in the corral and fed and watered them. Then we stored our gear along with the elk meat in a large tent. Finally, we made our way to the warm, dry travel trailers. We were cold, tired, and hungry.

Big Dave made us all forget that when he whipped up his favorite hot breakfast, sourdough pancakes. I had never had them before and o this day they remain my favorite breakfast, especially after a cold, snowy, ordeal like we had gone through to reach our base camp.

My Christmas gift to you is his recipe for sourdough

starter, the one ingredient necessary for sourdough pancakes. Over the years I kept my starter in a small ceramic pot with a sealed top.

Big Dave's sourdough starter:

Boil some potatoes and save the potato water. Use two cups of lukewarm potato water and mix with enough flour to make a thick dough. Place this mixture into a ceramic crock, cover it, and let it sit and ferment for a few days.

Now you have your sourdough starter.

If you want Big Dave's recipe for sourdough pancakes, email me at rwcallis@aol.com and ask for the recipe. I will email it to you.

THE END

HOME

Snow flurries were falling as Henry Conrad pulled his aged Subaru station wagon into the company parking lot. As usual, Henry had arrived early for work. He had made a lifelong habit of starting work early so he could get things done and organized before the phones started ringing and the emails began pouring in.

The parking lot was almost empty, even at seven o'clock in the morning. It was December 23rd and a Friday, and many employees of the company had found some way, legal or illegal, to skip work on the Friday before Christmas.

As Henry stepped out of his warm car and into the cold, windy parking lot, he paused to extract his briefcase from the back seat. As he closed the car door, he found himself shivering at the cold even though he wore a warm wool topcoat with a suit underneath it. It was cold for December, and the snow and wind made it seem even colder.

Henry made his way to the front of the building. It was a large, five story modern concrete and steel monolith with tons of windows. The company had built it on a small piece of farmland surrounded by undeveloped wooded land. The idea was to provide a serene environment and encourage creative thought among its workers. The company was one of the larger and fastest growing software companies in the United States. The building had been constructed during the Dot-Com period when all forms of software and hardware companies were booming. The building had never filled up before the economic bust came and since then there had been fewer and fewer cars in the company parking lot.

Henry had managed to survive the Dot-Com bust because he was a good software engineer, and he was hard working and creative. He came to work early, and he stayed late. He worked on weekends and even holidays when he had a deadline to meet and with few engineers, he almost always had a deadline to meet. He knew he had missed far too many birthdays and school plays and recitals, but he was sure his family understood that it was his job to provide a good living for them.

He inserted his magnetic card in the security card slot by the front door and waited until the door automatically unlocked and opened. He stepped into the lobby of the building and waved to Fred, the old heavy-set security guard. Fred was always cheerful and waved and usually greeted every employee by name. He was a retired cop who didn't make enough on his police pension to get buy so he had become a security guard at age sixty-two. Today Fred didn't bother to look up or acknowledge Henry's presence in the lobby. Henry wasn't sure if Fred was reading the morning paper or watching a security screen intently. While it was odd for Fred not to notice someone who entered the lobby, maybe it was just one of those things. Henry entered a waiting elevator and was soon whisked to the third floor where his office was located.

Henry emerged from the elevator and walked down the

hall to his office. He entered the security code in the device on the door of his office. The red light in the lock turned to green and he heard the lock click open. As he stepped inside his office, the lights automatically sensed his presence and turned themselves on. He took off his topcoat and suitcoat and hung them on a hook on the back of the office door. He then sat down at his desk and turned on his computer. After he placed a finger on a flat sensor, the system identified him, and his computer began to come online.

He got up and walked to the nearby employee lounge. He grabbed a clean coffee mug and tapped out the appropriate buttons on the coffee machine which promptly began to brew exactly one cup of large, decaf coffee slightly favored with vanilla.

He took his coffee mug from the machine, added cream and sugar, and then used a stir stick to mix it. Then he headed back to his office.

Back at his desk, He idly stirred his coffee while he went through his current too-do list. He had three projects underway and one of them was almost finished. He planned to finish that project and get a good start on the second one. By that time it should be midday and he'd take a half-hour break for lunch.

By mid-morning, he had finished his first project and forwarded it as an email attachment to his supervisor. He decided to hit the restroom before he started the new project and was surprised to see almost no one in any of the offices on his floor even though it was the middle of the morning.

When he finished his business in the restroom, he stopped at a sink to wash his hands. Then he used the cold-water faucet and splashed a little cold water on his face. As he dried his face with a paper towel, he found himself staring at his image in the large mirror behind the sink. He was fifty-six years old. His once lean frame now featured too much weight and he stooped instead of standing up straight. His formerly lean face was fleshy. His black hair was now streaked with grey, and his once smooth face was marked with wrinkles. His eyes were bloodshot, even with the clear contact lenses he wore. He looked older than he was, and he looked tired. Henry was a man worn down by life.

He closed his eyes and when he reopened them, nothing in the mirror had changed. He was still old and tired. He wearily turned and headed back to his office and the waiting project.

Before he went back to his office he stopped at the lounge and got a second cup of coffee. He thought it odd that the lounge was empty. He also noticed that unlike any other holiday, there were no plates of cookies or Christmas candy setting on the counter of the lounge.

On the way back to his office, he saw that only two other employees were in their offices. The rest of the offices on his floor were dark and empty. He shrugged and returned to his office. In his absence, his computer had gone into hibernation. He hit the return key to wake up the computer and turned in his chair to pick up his coffee cup. He had the cup halfway to his mouth when an urgent email flashed on his screen, and he froze as he read the contents.

Slowly he set the coffee mug down and stared at his screen, his eyes seeing, but his brain was disbelieving.

There in clear electronic letters, done in bold, no less, was an email to him from Human resources.

From: Human Resources
To: Henry Conrad

As of noon today, your employment with the company is terminated. Please remove all your personal effects from your office and leave your ID badge and your magnetic access card with the security guard in the lobby. He will have you sign a release form and give you a final paycheck. Boxes for personal possessions are available in the closet next to the elevator. You do not need to return the boxes.

Happy Holidays.

Henry was stunned. He couldn't believe his eyes. He had been with the company for almost six years. He had never been late, never called in sick, and had always finished his projects before his deadlines. How could this be? There had to be some mistake! He tried calling HR on the intercom. All he got was a voice mail message that the HR department was closed until the Monday after Christmas.

He slowly lowered the phone receiver and placed it back in the cradle. He finally realized that it truly was over. He had been fired! He had lost his job! He had no idea what he was going to tell his wife. How would he be able to face his family? How was a fifty-six-year-old software engineer going to find work in one of the worst markets in twenty years?

He slumped in his chair. He felt like someone had just punched him in his stomach and knocked the wind out of him. He leaned forward in his chair and struggled to breathe. The stress of the moment seemed to crush the air out of his lungs like there was a vice around his chest. He forced himself to relax and finally his breathing slowly returned to normal. He laid his head on top of his arms and rested them on his desktop.

About twenty minutes passed. Henry pulled himself upright in his chair. The sleeves of his dress shirt were damp from his tears. He felt ashamed of his tears and the fear he felt though his entire body. He was truly afraid. He had debts. He had a family to provide for and he had no idea where to turn or what to do. For the first time in his life, he thought about suicide. Never had he felt so helpless or lost.

Finally, he got to his feet and walked down the hall to the closed with the boxes stored in it. There were only four boxes left. He took one back to his office and began filling it with his mementos and personal items. Most of them were pictures of his wife Nancy and their two children Fran and Tim. Both were now out of college and married and they had come to visit their parents for Christmas. They and their families were at home with his wife, waiting for him to return. How would he face them?

When the elevator deposited him at the main floor lobby, he would see a co-worker, Wally Sherman, at Fred's desk in the center of the lobby. He was signing a form. A cardboard box was on the floor next to him.

He watched as Welly gave Fred back the signed form, his ID badge, and building pass. Fred handed Wally a long white envelope with Wally's name on it. Wally left immediately without even a glance at Henry.

He stepped up to the guard's desk. Fred silently handed him a form on a clipboard along with a pen. Henry signed the form and returned it along with his ID badge and his building pass. Fred then handed him an envelope with Henry's name on it. Fred looked up at Henry with pity in his eyes, but he remained silent.

Henry trudged to the front door carrying his box and his briefcase. Just before he reached out to open the door, he heard Fred speak. "Good luck, Henry."

Henry smiled briefly and turned to wave back at Fred. Then he was out the door.

The snow and wind had picked up and Henry hurried to his car. He didn't know what he was going to tell Nancy, but now he just wanted to get home. He had no idea what he was going to do then, but he knew if he could just get home, he could figure something out.

Henry lived about fifteen miles from the office in a subdivision located in the country. The highway that passed near his subdivision had been almost empty of cars when he came to work. Now the highway was snow covered and full of people in their vehicles trying to get home to their families. Because of the weather, the road was treacherous, and the heavy traffic made it worse. Henry was almost glad of the conditions as he had to focus on his driving and that left little time to worry about his current situation and how he was going to explain to his wife and children that he had been fired.

About fifteen minutes later he had only traveled about two miles, and he was getting frustrated. UP ahead was a turn-off to a country road he was pretty sure would provide him with a way around the snowbound traffic jam he was currently in. He thought he had taken that road before, but he wasn't positive.

As soon as he neared the turnoff, he pulled the Subaru

to the right side of the road and went down the snow-covered shoulder until he got to the junction. He could tell that snow was coming down harder, but he had confidence in the all-wheel drive of the old Subaru.

As he drove, the snow was blowing sideways and making visibility exceedingly difficult. He could hardly make out the outline of the road and he could see nothing that he recognized on either side of the road. He slowed the Subaru's speed to little more than a crawl. He knew he was still on the road, but he had no idea of exactly where he was.

Then he heard the engine of the Subaru begin to cough and shake and it finally wheezed and stopped as it exhaled exhaust gas as though it was the car's dying breath. The car had stopped on the side of the road with snow swirling all around it. Henry could not see for more than ten yards in any direction. He began to panic and then talked himself into focusing on his breathing until he felt normal again. He couldn't believe it. Could the day get any worse? He tried his cell phone. He got a low battery image and got no signal!

Then he remembered he kept his snow boots in the back seat of the Subaru. He grabbed them, removed his dress shoes, and replaced them with his warm, insulated boots. If he had to walk, at least he was prepared.

He sat in the car for a while. He was not sure exactly how long. The snow had begun to pile up on the hood of the Subaru. The next thing he knew a pickup truck had pulled up next to his stalled car and stopped.

Henry got out of the car and the driver of the truck rolled down the passenger side window.

"Need some help, mister?"

The driver was an elderly man. He was short, stocky, and

mostly bald with a few wisps of white hair rowing around the side of his head. He had a rather stern countenance but belied that with a wide grin and a sparkle in his eyes that reflected in the wire rimmed glasses he wore.

"You bet," said Henry. "Can I get a lift to the nearest service station?"

"Absolutely. I'm headed to town and will go right by Johnson's Mobil Gas Station. Hope in," he replied.

Henry soon found himself seated on the passenger side of an old pickup truck. The truck was in very good shape and the warm air from the truck's heater was a welcome reminder it had been getting cold in the motionless Subaru.

The old man drove effortlessly through the storm and by the time he pulled into Johnson's Mobil Gas Station, the snow had almost stopped. As Henry exited the truck and watched it pull out of the service station lot, he saw something curious. ON the side of the truck bed, just behind the cab, the old man had painted "EW 3450" and below that "T.P. Main & Sons." Henry couldn't remember seeing anything like that on a pickup truck since he was a child. Back in those days, the farmers painted the estimated weight of the truck so they could tell the weights of load of gain by pulling onto a scale, taking that weight, and subtracting the estimated weight of the truck to get the weight of the load. They also painted their names and whether they had sons. In an era when labor was important to the family farm, the more sons a farmer had the better.

Henry entered the small office of the service station, introduced himself and explained his plight to the manager, a short bald man named Harland.

"Well Mr. Conrad, Hank is out right now with the truck,

but he should be back pretty soon," said Harland. "As you can see, we're kind of busy here and I can't spare anyone else. You're welcome to wait here in the office and help yourself to the coffee. It ain't great, but it's hot."

By the time Henry had finished the strong black coffee, Hank had returned with the truck. He talked briefly to Harland and then quickly introduced himself to Henry.

Hank was about eighteen years old. He had a rangy build and was as tall as Henry. He had black hair, dark brown eyes, and an engaging smile. He wore work boots, jeans, and a navy high school letterman's jacket topped off with a blue and gold stocking cap. He took off his work gloves to shake hands with Henry.

"Nice to meet you, Mr. Conrad. Sorry to hear about your car problems. This storm and the cold have created a lot of problems. I've been out jump starting and pushing cars since seven this morning," said Hank.

"Nice to meet you, Hank. I sure appreciate you being able to help me."

"What seems to be wrong with your car, Mr. Conrad?" asked Hank.

"I'm not sure. It just coughed a few times and the engine died," replied Henry.

"Do you maybe run out of gas?" asked Hank.

"No, I checked, and the gauge showed I had almost a full tank," replied Henry.

"Could be a gas line freeze. We get a lot of those when it gets cold real sudden like. Don't worry sir. We can take care of whatever it is," said Hank.

Hank went to the old black wall phone and pulled several

sheets of paper from a hook on the wall next to it. After reading them, he turned to Henry.

"Mr. Conrad, I've got a few other jobs that are ahead of you. You can stay here, or you can ride with me. If you ride with me, we can head to your ca as soon as I finish the other jobs," said Hank.

Henry wanted to get home as soon as possible, and he agreed to ride with Hank. They headed outside for Hank's truck.

Hank saw Henry stop and stare and he laughed.

"It's old, but it's tough and it always gets the job done," said Hank. The truck was an old Willy's Jeep with a winch and tow hitch.

They climbed in the old Jeep and headed out. The snow had stopped, and the sun was trying to push its way through the cloud cover. The temperature was still cold, but it was warmer than Henry remembered.

Their first stop was in front of a modest two-story house. Hank pulled up next to a snow-covered old Chevrolet. A middle-aged lady was trying to get the snow off the car with a long-handled broom.

"Here, Mrs. Huber, let me get that for you," said Hank. He quickly cleared the snow off the car and then hooked up the charger battery on the Jeep to Mrs. Huber's Chevrolet. He quickly got the engine started and left the car running. Hank told Mrs. Huber Harland would send her a bill. She thanked Hank and gave him a hug. Hank slid back into the Jeep, and they were off to the next stop.

Hank jump started an Oldsmobile for Mrs. Sanders in front of the Post Office and then pulled Mrs. Olson's Ford station wagon out of the ditch by her driveway.

"I'm so embarrassed. I can't believe I drove off the driveway and into the ditch," she said. She also thanked Hank profusely and gave him a hug.

The little town had no stoplight and was built around a large town square. Through the middle of the square was a railroad train track with crossing gates guarding the tracks.

On their next pass-through downtown, a freight train with a lot of coal cars was slowly pushing its way through the town square. While they were stopped at the crossing gate, three teenage boys walked by on the snowy sidewalk.

"Hey, Hank. What's up?" said a tall blonde boy.

"Hey, Willie. Not much, just workin'," responded Hank.

"Better you than me," retorted Willie.

Hank just laughed in response.

The boys continued on their way.

Hank's next stop was at the auto supply store to pick up a part for Harland. Henry followed Hank into the store. Inside, the place looked like something out of the 1960's with dim overhead lights and shelves and shelves of parts.

"How's it goin'" Hank?" said a tall lanky man wearing and set for worn big overalls.

"Goin' great, Slim. I'm here to pick up a generator for Harland," said Hank.

"Got it right here. We were lucky to have it on hand. It's for one of them foreign cars. A Jap one I think," said Slim.

Hank signed for the part.

"Thanks Slim," said Hank and they were out the door.

When they were back in the jeep, Hank started the engine. Hank turned to face Henry. "I hate to add any delay to your day, but I need to stop and say hi to my mom," he said.

"Sure," replied Henry with a puzzled look on his face.

Hank parked in front of the First National Bank. Henry accompanied Hank inside. The interior of the bank was very old like something you would see in the 1950's. Hank stepped up to one of the teller windows and received a smile from the attractive middle-aged teller. Henry looked up at her and he was stunned. She was the spitting image of his mother when she was about fifty years old. He then turned and slowly looked around the bank. It looked eerily like the bank his mother had worked in when he was a boy and she was a single parent, trying to make a living for her family while she was working as a bank teller.

Hank pulled Henry out of his thoughts by taking him by the arm and pulling him up to the teller position manned by Hank's mother.

"Mom, this is Mr. Conrad. He's having some car trouble, so I am taking him back out to the blacktop to help him get it running. Mr. Conrad, this is my mom."

Hank's mother smiled and said, "Pleased to meet you Mr. Conrad," as she extended her hand. Henry hesitated and then reached out and took her hands in his. Her touch felt warm and comforting. It made him feel warm and safe.

"You make sure Mr. Conrad gets home to his family, Hank," said his mother.

"I will, mom. See you tonight," said Hank.

The next thing Henry knew, they were back in the old jeep and Henry had started the engine. As they pulled away from the bank, Henry turned to Hank and asked him, "What does your father do, Hank?"

"My dad is dead. He died of injuries he had in the war," said Hank softly.

Henry's heart almost stopped. His father had died of a

blood clot due to surgery for injuries in World War II. That meant Hank's mother was a single parent, just like Henry's.

"Your car is the next stop, Mr. Conrad," said Hank. "I need to stop at home and get some fresh work gloves. These gloves are wet and it's cold out."

Hank pulled the old jeep up in front of a modest frame two-story home.

"I'll just be a minute, Mr. Conrad," said Hank as he jumped out of the still running jeep.

Henry stared at the house. Before him was an exact duplicate of the simple home he had grown up in. Every detail was the same. The small front porch was decorated with a real evergreen garland and outdoor Christmas lights. ON the front door was a large evergreen wreath with a bright red box. It was exactly as his mother had decorated their front porch every year when he was a boy.

Henry was shaken out of his self-induced trance by Hank jerking open the truck door and jumping back into the driver's seat.

Then they headed past the edge of town and Hank turned onto a narrow blacktop road. As they drove the clouds covered up the sun and wisps of fog began to surround the narrow blacktop.

Henry found his curiosity about what he had just experienced overwhelming his sense of propriety.

"With your father gone, I assume it has been pretty tough for you and your mother?" Henry said.

"Oh no, Mr. Conrad. My mom, my sister and I have each other. We're a family and we have tons of family and friends around us. Our neighbors, the people we work for, all of them look out for us. My mom always tells us that no one who has family and friends is ever poor or alone," said Hank.

Henry had no response. As they drove down the black top road the weather quickly changed from fairly foggy to quite foggy and Henk turned on the headlights of the old Willys.

The next thing Henry saw was his old Subaru as they pulled up next to it.

"Do you have the keys, Mr. Conrad?" asked Hank.

"Of course, Hank. Here they are," said Henry as he got out of the truck and handed the keys to Hank.

Hank jumped into the driver's seat of the Subaru and inserted the key in the ignition. He turned it and the engine leaped to life.

"Just like I thought, Mr. Conrad. It was probably a gas line frozen, and the sun came out and it melted. I'd be careful of where I buy my gas in the future," said Hank.

Henry stood there and stared in amazement. He waited until Hank got out of the car and then he sat in the Subaru's driver's seat. He deliberately turned the ignition off and then turned it back on. The engine roared to life.

Henry turned to look out the driver's door window to speak to Hank.

But Hank was gone. So was the old Willys. Only a few wisps of fog marked the spot where Henry had last seen Hank and the Jeep.

Henry sat there in the Subaru. The only sound he could hear was the car's engine. He shut the engine off. Then he was surrounded by silence and the ghostly wisps of fog around the car.

What had happened to him? Was it real? Had he imagined it? Had he fallen asleep and dreamed it?

He sat there for several minutes in the silence of the Subaru's interior until he remembered what Hank had told him.

"No one who has family and friends is ever poor or alone."

Henry turned the ignition key and started the car. The fog was gone, and the sun had returned. Tehe snow on the blacktop road was melting. Tomorrow is Christmas Eve. His wife and family were waiting for him. It was time to go home.

THE END

GETTING OFF THE BENCH

CHAPTER ONE

Beverly Calhoun carried her dirty breakfast dishes to the dishwasher, dodging between her two cocker spaniels, Barney, and Buzzard. As soon as she had the machine loaded, she put in the soap tablet, closed the door, and hit the start button. Then she hit the grind button on her coffee maker, and it promptly filled the kitchen with the sound of grinding coffee beans followed by a sweet aroma. As she waited for the coffee to be made, she contemplated the two baskets of dirty laundry that stood like sentinels to the door leading to the laundry room.

The volume of laundry had risen only slightly since her brother Tom had come to live with Bev and her husband. Tom's monk like existence never seemed to create much in the way of dirty clothes. How was that possible, she wondered?

She fed the dogs who until then had followed her every move, causing her to walk carefully so as not to trip over one of the moving furry obstacles. Her importance had been trumped by mere dog food. She enjoyed the moment, knowing that as soon as they had wolfed down the dog food they would be back at her heels, like two moving shadows.

She poured herself a cup of fresh coffee and sat on a chair at the kitchen table. It had been almost a month since she and her husband Tip had decided to go rescue her depressed brother before he either hurt or killed himself through sheer neglect.

Tip, whose real name was Theopolis Calhoun, was a successful lawyer in the small Illinois town of Galva, population 2,868 friendly folks and two soreheads. Tip had taken over his father's law practice when his mother had decided she had seen enough Illinois winters and talked her husband into retiring and moving to Florida. Tip's father had finally given in and now Tip owned the law practice and his parents' old two-story turn-of-the-century large house across from Wiley Park.

Wiley Park was named after the small town's founding family and until the new park district built a new park with a swimming pool and ball parks, it was the largest park in the small town. Wiley Park was the equivalent of six square blocks and was blessed with century-old trees. At its center was a small bandstand. At the south end was a small brick housing the public restrooms. At the northeast end of the park was a playground area dominated by an asphalt basketball court that contained two basketballs courts, side by side. The backboards were the traditional steel painted white and the rims held nets of chain link rather than the more fragile nylon cord.

Bev and Tip's house was directly across the street from the basketball courts. In years past, there had been an elementary school located on the east side of the park. Due to a declining population, the school had been closed years before. Now the old school building housed the city's' offices. Both the playground and basketball courts experienced less use than when they bordered the school, but they still attracted activity.

As Bev rose to get a second cup of coffee, she looked out the window over her sink into her fenced back yard. The two dogs had gone down into the basement where they could exit the house through a doggie door and play in the back yard. The two dogs were chasing each other and having a good time outside.

Bev sat down with her fresh cup of coffee. She remembered that rainy day in early May when she and Tip had driven to Des Moines towing a rented U-Haul trailer. When they reached her brother's apartment, she found the door unlocked and they just walked in. The place was a mess. Clothes and newspapers littered the floor and furniture. The kitchen was a toxic waste site. Dirty dishes and pots and pans were covered with gunk that defied description. It looked like the gunk, mated with other goo, and produced more gunk as offspring. The smell was appalling.

She found her brother in a pair of dirty pajamas and a tattered bathrobe asleep in a recliner located in front of a television that showed nothing but an electronically created snowstorm. She checked the tv. It was on a cable system. Her brother had probably not paid the cable bill and it had been shut off for nonpayment.

Her brother was thin, unshaven, and smelly. He awoke and was not happy to see his only sister. Tip had appeared with a box of large, extra-strength garbage bags. Bev had Tip get her brother up and introduce him to the bathroom and the shower. She began dividing his possessions into two piles. She mentally labeled the piles as Keep and Toss.

She and Tip and her brother spent the next four hours

hauling bags from the Keep pile into the trailer and bags from the Toss pile into the dumpster. Her brother Tom's paltry amount of decent furniture went into the trailer. Everything else went into the dumpster.

When they were finished, her brother Tom was presentable and seated in the front passenger seat of their SUV. The trailer was full. Bev drove the SUV straight back to Galva with Tip following driving Tom's yellow Jeep Wrangler. The Jeep had not been driven in a while and it took several tries to get it started. Once it was started, the Jeep's engine seemed to run smoothly.

It was a long drive back to Galva. Bev deposited Tom in the guest room across the hall from the master bedroom and they put his garbage bags from the Keep pile in the back porch off the kitchen. His small amount of furniture went into the garage.

For the next month Tom slept in every day. He came downstairs for meals and barely spoke for the first week. Then he began to stay in the kitchen after breakfast and watch some television, read the paper, and talk to his sister.

Over the last month he had gained weight and begun to regain some of the color in his face. At Bev's insistence, he showered and shaved every day and began to look more like the brother she had always known.

She took hope in his small steps of progress, but it hurt her to see how unlike the brother she had known that he had become.

She smiled as she thought of her big brother. He had been active and full of life as a boy growing up in Galva. He worked hard, played hard, and had grown from a boy into a young man. He had played varsity sports and had hung out with his friends and done all the things a young man in a small town is able to do. When he graduated from Galva High School and went on to college, she knew he would do well. Tm had graduated from college and taken a job with a brokerage firm in Des Moines as a stockbroker. He had done well and married a girl from Des Moines he had met at a party. She was a CPA and had worked for a large accounting firm. They had no children as both were deeply involved in their careers. Then, one day after almost twelve years of marriage, he had felt sick at work and decided to go home. He had stopped at a drug store on the way home and picked up some over-the-counter meds for the flu. He was kicking himself for not getting a flu shot earlier that year. He had surprised his wife at home. She was supposed to be at work. He found her in bed with one of her co-workers.

Tom moved out and into a small apartment with a few possessions. The divorce was quick and painless. The emotional fall out was not. He could not concentrate at work. At first his boss was sympathetic and gave him time off. But when Tom began to forget appointments with clients or neglect to execute stock orders and did not return phone calls, his boss finally lost patience and fired him.

Tom was depressed and found himself unable to function. He lived like a hermit in his apartment and depended on food delivery for subsistence. He began to live in self-imposed squalor. Bev had visited him and had become alarmed. Finally, she decided to rescue him from himself, and Tip had agreed to help.

CHAPTER TWO

Bev heard Tom's footsteps on the stairs. He was shaved and dressed in a t-shirt and jeans. His feet were bare. His dark curly hair was a little unruly as though he had run a brush through it and given up.

Tom was about six foot three inches tall. He had broad shoulders and now weighed about one hundred and eighty pounds. He had gained almost twenty pounds since his rescue and was still about twenty pounds under his normal weight. He had almost black hair and was almost back to his normal dark complexion. He had rugged good looks. He also had a great smile, but Bev had not seen that trademark smile since his breakup with his wife.

She poured him a cup of coffee and he helped himself to a bowl of dry cereal and a glass of orange juice. This was huge progress from when he had first arrived, and Bev had to literally force food down his throat. When breakfast was over, he helped clear the table and then took a seat in the living room and began to read the morning newspaper.

When Bev returned from grocery shopping, she found him watching a game show on television in the living room.

"It's a nice day out, Tom. Why don't we sit out on the front porch?" she asked.

Tom nodded his agreement and they moved to the front porch. The porch was large and ran the full width of the house. The roof line of the house came down and extended over the porch giving the occupants shade from the sun and shelter from the rain and snow. The porch contained large wicker chairs complete with cushions. They sat and talked. Well, Bev did most of the talking and as she ran on about what was happening in Galva, Tom would nod his head to acknowledge he had heard her but didn't add anything to the conversation.

Tom appreciated all his sister had done for him, but he still felt like he was being smothered by a feeling of hopelessness and despair that made him feel like his arms and legs were made out of lead. He who had always been active felt no sense of purpose or ambition. In his last days at work, he could not get himself to function in his job. He could barely force himself to eat. At times he had just wanted to fall asleep and never wake up. Now that he was at his sister's house he felt better, but he still felt empty inside.

After Bev went inside the house to start preparing supper, Tom found himself studying the park across the street. The park had been planted with several varieties of trees over a century ago. The trees towered above the grass below them and provided an immense amount of shade. He could make out what he thought were oak and maple trees, but he was unsure of the rest. He could see several squirrels bounding over their large network of branches high in the air and occasionally they would come down to the ground and then scamper through the lush green grass.

He could also see and hear several varieties of birds. Bev had placed a bird bath on the front lawn, and it was popular with an entire neighborhood of birds, including those who had made the park their home. The robins not only drank the water, but they also liked to get in the bird bath and use their wings to give themselves a bath. Tom smiled at their antics. Although he didn't realize it, this was the first time he had smiled for quite a while.

He heard a shout and looked up from the scene at the birdbath. Over in the park two young boys had arrived at the basketball court and were shooting baskets. One was tall and lanky with light skin and bright red hair. Tom immediately dubbed him "Red." The other boy was short and slightly stocky but had arms that seemed to belong to a taller boy. He shot the basketball with his left hand, so Tom decided to call him "Lefty."

Red and Lefty started out playing a game of what Tom was sure was HORSE. One player would make a shot and the other player had to match the same shot. If he missed, he got a letter. The players took turns originating a shot. When a player accumulated all the letters to spell HORSE, he was the loser. As Tom watched the two plays shoot baskets, they played about four games of HORSE. Each of them won two games. Then they began to play a basic game of twenty-one. Each of them took turns playing offense against the other. If one made a basket, then the other boy took the ball on offense until one of them had a combined score of twenty-one or more. Both boys had good speed and quickness although Lefty was a bit quicker, but Red could jump higher. Lefty used his speed to get around Red, but on several occasions, Red was able to block Lefty's shot even though Lefty had beaten him to the basket off the dribble.

Then an old pickup truck pulled up next to the basketball court and four more young boys piled out and joined Lefty and Red. After a brief time spent shooting baskets, the boys divided up into two teams of three against three. After watching them for a while, Tom was able to give each of them a nickname so he could remember who was who.

One of the boys was about six feet tall, but powerfully built. He was strong and it showed that he was able to rip a rebound away from Red. He was also a powerful jumper and was taking rebounds right off the rim of the basket. He also moved quickly, but Tom soon saw he was a poor shooter. His short jump shots were banging off the rim or the backboard. Tom promptly named him "Brick."

Another of the boys was tall and slim, almost skinny. He moved well but seemed a bit tentative. Tom named him "Toothpick" or "Pick" for short.

The third boy was very tall, but very awkward. He was obviously growing fast and having trouble getting all his parts moving in the same direction. Tom decided to call him "Lurch."

The fourth boy was short, thin, and lightning fast. He had very quick feet and even quicker hands. He had a quick burst of speed that belied his small stature. Tom labeled the small fast kid, "Speedy."

So now there were six players on the court. To Tom, they had become Lefty, Red, Brick, Pick, Lurch and Speedy. As they played, he found himself leaning forward in his chair watching their every move. After about an hour Tom felt he had been able to figure out their strengths and weaknesses. They were pretty good players, but they did not pass the ball very well. They did not use screens well, and they were not strong defenders. His personal review of the six boys was cut short by his sister summons to supper. He reluctantly left his porch seat to join his sister and brother-in-law for dinner

CHAPTER THREE

Bev noticed something was different about her brother. He seemed more alert. He seemed to listen to the dinner time conversation with interest. Then, when Tip related a funny story about one of his clients, Tom actually laughed out loud. She had no idea what caused it, but she was secretly delighted. This was progress. This gave her hope.

The next day Tom came down early to join Bev and Tip for breakfast. He was showered, shaven, and dressed in a T-shirt and sweatpants. And he was wearing socks and tennis shoes. She couldn't remember the last time he had not been barefoot. As they finished breakfast, Tom asked a strange question.

"Do we have a basketball around here?" he asked.

Both Bev and Tip looked up from their coffee in surprise.

"No, we don't," responded Tip. "But I believe here was one in that stuff of yours we stored out in the garage."

Tom thanked Tip and again surprised his sister by breaking into a smile.

After Tip left for the office and Bev was clearing the breakfast dishes off the table, she turned to see Tom cleaning off dishes and putting them in the dishwasher. This was a first for him.

Then Tom headed out the door to the garage. After about fifteen minutes he emerged with a worn and somewhat flat basketball. "Do we have an air pump, Sis?" Tom asked.

"In the garage, on the workbench in the back," she answered.

Pretty soon he emerged from the garage bouncing the ball on the driveway. Then he headed out to the street and across it to the park basketball court.

Tom started out slowly, with lay-ups and short shots. After about twenty minutes he stopped to rest. He was wet with sweat, and he felt weak. This was the result of cheating his body with a poor diet and no exercise for almost four months and his body was protesting.

After resting on a park bench near the court, he returned and began a series of basic drills that he had not performed since he was a high school varsity player in this same small town.

After two hours he returned to the house, showered, changed clothes, and took a nap. Bev woke him and told him lunch was ready. After lunch he asked her if he had a small notebook she could spare. She produced a small spiral notebook after a few minutes searching in one of her kitchen drawers. Tom took the notebook and a pencil out to the front porch and began writing some notes. He sat back in his chair and drank a can of Coke while he watched the squirrels and birds in the park along with the occasional mother and her children.

When the six boys arrived about four in the afternoon, he sat up in his chair and watched intently as they played. He looked down occasionally to write something in his notebook. When the boys finally quit the court, he returned inside the house, read the newspaper, and watched some television.

The next day he repeated this routine and this time he went back to the court after supper and shot baskets until it became dark.

This soon became his daily routine. He shot baskets in the morning and evening and for about two hours every late afternoon he watched the six boys play and he took notes.

Tom seemed disappointed when Sunday came, and the boys did not show up. But on Monday, they were back and so was he with his notebook.

After two weeks of this he changed his routine. His morning practices became more intense, and he finished them by jogging around the perimeter of the park. His appetite increased and he became more animated when talking to Bev and Tip. He offered to mow the lawn and did so with relish and careful attention to detail.

After week three, he changed his routine again. Tom moved off the front porch to the park bench located about twenty yards from the basketball court. The first day the boys ignored him, but they did say hello as they arrived and then began playing against each other. Tom sat, watched, and took notes.

On the third day of Tom's move to the park bench, Brick arrived long before any of his friends. He said Hello to Tom and Tom responded. Then Brick asked, "What are you writing down in that notebook, mister?"

Tom smiled. "Well, son, I'm taking notes on you and your five friends as to how you play basketball."

"Why are you doin' that?" asked a puzzled-looking Brick.

"I've been watching you boys play for several weeks and

decided to keep track of what you are doing right and what you could use some more work on," responded Tom.

"You're takin' notes on us?" asked Brick incredulously. "Are you a scout or a coach?"

"Nope. I'm just an old ballplayer who likes to watch the game no matter where they play it," replied Tom.

"You played basketball?" asked a surprised Brick.

"I lettered playing basketball for Galva High School for three years," said Tom.

"Wow. When was that?" asked Brick.

"A long time ago, son. Long before your time," said a smiling Tom.

"So, what did you write in that book of yours about me?" asked a curious Brick.

Tom grinned. "You are a strong kid. You can jump and rebound, and you play decent defense. You have trouble with your shot."

Brick seemed surprised by Tom's assessment. He paused for a moment and then spoke up. "You're right. How come I can't shoot like the other guys?"

Tom paused before he answered the young man's question. Finally, he said, "You seem to heave the ball at the basket rather than shoot it."

"I do?" said a surprised Brick.

"Yes, you do. Show me how you hold the ball with your hands when you get ready to shoot the ball," said Tom.

After watching how Brick gripped the ball, Tom repositioned Brick's fingers and then adjusted how he held the ball. Finally, he adjusted Brick's shooting motion with his arms and then his follow through.

"Good shooters are balanced," said Tom. "They are

squared up to the basket with their shoulders, and they use one hand to hold or steady the ball and one hand to actually shoot the ball. Then they have a smooth motion of shooting, and they follow through with their shot after they have released the ball."

"Can you show me?" asked Brick.

Tom hesitated for a moment. Then he took the basketball, spun it in his hands, pivoted toward the basket and then smoothly placed the ball properly in his hands and took a fifteen-foot jump shot that went cleanly through the basket.

"How did you do that?" asked Brick.

Tom smiled and spent the next fifteen minutes showing Brick how to hold the ball and then keep a consistent shooting motion with his arms. Brick took shot after shot and finally began to see the ball fall through the hoop with consistency.

Shortly after that, the other five boys arrived. Brick introduced them all to Tom and told them about Tom helping him with his shot.

"He has no shot," said Lefty. "He shoots like a blacksmith. He is more likely to punch a hole through the backboard with the ball than to make basket."

"Let's see," said a smiling Tom. He tossed the ball to Brick.

Brick's first shot bounced off the rim and the other five boys hooted at his miss. Brick took a deep breath and squared up his shoulders as Tom had taught him to and smoothly released the ball on a jump shot. The shot went cleanly through the basket. The other four boys all began yelling and pummeling Brick with their hands.

"How did you teach him to do that?" asked a puzzled-looking Lefty.

"He watched us and took notes and used them to show me what I was doing wrong," said Brick. "He also has nicknames for each of us."

"You gave us nicknames?" asked Pick.

"I gave you nicknames because I didn't know your real names, and it was easier to keep track of you when I watched you play," said Tom.

"He played varsity for Galva for three years when he was a kid," said Brick.

Tom smiled at the thought of "when he was a kid." That did seem a long time ago.

"Can you help the rest of us with our game?" asked Lefty.

"I can try, Lefty, but you have to want to learn, or it will be a waste of time," replied Tom.

"My nickname is Lefty. Cool," said Lefty.

The rest of the boys wanted to learn their nicknames and Tom told them the names he used to keep track of them. All six of them seemed delighted with their nicknames and immediately began using them on each other.

Then Tom asked each boy to tell him a little bit about themselves and why they wanted to play basketball. In turn they each told him and then asked him to tell them about his team when he played for Galva. Tom took a small amount of pleasure in recounting those teams. He remembered how much he had enjoyed playing on those teams and how much that had meant to him at the time.

Tom learned that the five boys were all sophomores and were likely to be reserves on the next year's team, if they managed to make the team. They could play on the

Frosh-Soph team but were unlikely to even dress for varsity home games.

Tom showed them some basic drills and had them work on them until it was time for them to go home. Tom promised to be back the next day and work with each of them on the things they needed help with.

CHAPTER FOUR

Each day for the rest of the summer, Tom worked with the six boys for about two hours every afternoon. After the sessions began, the boys decided to show up on Sundays as well. They came each day after they got off work from their summer jobs. During this time, Tom continued to increase his personal drills and to run greater distances. He regained the weight he had lost and began to build a solid base of muscle tone. His skin regained its color and began to tan under the hot, Illinois summer sun. The boys got better and better. They learned to fake and shoot or pass. They learned to set and use good screens. They shot with their left hands when they approached the basket from the left side on the baseline. They learned to effectively screen out on rebounds using their bodies as shields. They also learned to play good defense using their feet and hands rather than relying mostly on their hands.

Stick and Lurch became skilled at playing with their backs to the basket. Lefty and Speedy improved their ball handling and passing skills. Speedy discovered how the cross-over dribble gave him a step on the defender and his speed and quickness took care of the rest. Red was a good baseline player, and he could shoot well from the outside.

He could also take the ball to the hoop with authority. Brick was a good inside player. His shot range was about twelve feet and in, but he worked on a hook shot with Tom and soon he could shoot it well with either hand from as far out as fifteen feet. He also became good at driving to the basket and using either his left or his right hand to shoot.

Most of all, they learned to play well together. At the end of the summer, Tom invited all six boys over to his sister's house to watch a movie on DVD. He selected the movie "Hoosiers." As the boys watched the movie, drinking soft drinks and eating popcorn, Tom would pause the movie to show them a specific move and to make a specific point. When the movie was over the boys filed out and left for their respective homes. Tom cleaned up the empty pop cans and popcorn bowls while his sister watched and smiled.

The next day school started, and the boys continued to show up after school to play on the court in the park and Tom continued to teach them the game.

In late September Tip asked Tom to stop by his office at about ten in the morning.

Tom was not sure what Tip had in mind, but he showed up on time, dressed in a T-shirt and shorts. Tip asked him to have a seat in his office and then pulled out a folder. Tip explained that as a small-town lawyer, he handled a lot of estates. Normally they were older people, and their affairs were well organized and ordinary.

This estate was not ordinary. A couple in their late thirties had been killed in an auto accident and had left behind two minor children. A boy aged six and a girl aged four. Their aunt and uncle were to be the appointed guardians. Unlike most of Tip's clients, the couple had not only owned a great deal of life insurance, but they had also invested in a small company that had gone public and then had been acquired by an even bigger company. The estate for the two small children was over six million dollars. Under the terms of the wills a trust had been established with Tip as the trustee.

"I am uncomfortable with a trust this size without obtaining some expert help to manage the investing," said Tip. "I would oversee the investing and make the final decisions, but I would like some professional help in investing the money for the trust. I think your background as a stockbroker gives you the credential for the job. I can pay you a fee for your services which the trust provides for. Are you interested in the job?"

Tom was speechless. Finally, he managed to find his voice and he said, "I really thank you for this opportunity, but I haven't done anything in the market for over ten months."

"I doubt your skills have deserted you in just ten months. It would not take long for you to get up to speed on what is going on in the market. I talked to your former boss in Des Moines, and he said you would be perfect for the job." said Tip.

After a brief discussion on the terms and restrictions of the trust and the amount of the fee to be paid, Tom left Tip's office an hour later. He was no longer an unemployed person.

Tom quickly got up to speed on his investing opportunities for the trust. He bought a laptop computer and a printer and used the wireless component of his sisters' wireless system. Within two weeks the portfolio of the trust was established and doing well. Tip was pleased and so was the aunt and uncle who were the trustees for the two children. Tom's training sessions with the six boys ended in late October when the weather turned colder and unsuitable for outdoor basketball.

Word of Tom's success as an investment counselor spread and soon Tip had referred three retired farm couples who had old their farms and needed help with their investment of the sales proceeds. One day Tom took his long-neglected Jeep through the local self-service car wash on a warm day. After running the Jeep through the wash, he pulled out and parked by the side of the building so he could dry off the Jeep with some old towels he had borrowed from his sister.

As he bent over to dry off the wheels of the Jeep, he heard a voice from the past say, "I figgered old Tommy boy would end up workin' in a damned car wash."

Tom rose to his feet and turned to see a short, skinny unshaven man dressed up in an old army surplus coat and tattered blue jeans. On his feet were a pair of old worn tennis shoes.

"Yup. You still look like old Tommy Boy Main," said the man with a smile on his face.

"Jerry Hoxland!" said a surprised Tom.

"Was the last time I checked," said Jerry. "Course that was some time ago and things coulda' changed."

Tom grinned and stepped forward to give his old friend a hug, which was returned with true enthusiasm.

"Kinda chilly out here," said Tom. "You got time for a cup of coffee?"

"Time is all I got plenty of, Tommy Boy," replied Jerry.

They jumped in Tom's Jeep, and he drove down to Amy's café. Over several cups of coffee, Tom learned Jerry had joined the army after high school and ended up a tank gunner. He was part of the Gulf War, and his tank driver made a mistake and drove their tank into a canal. All the crew drowned, except Jerry. He made it up to the surface and a fellow soldier performed CPR on him until a medic showed up. After the war, Jerry was diagnosed with PTSD and discharged from the army with a disability allowance. He lived in the small house he grew up in. His mother had died of cancer and left the house to Jerry.

Jerry had no car, and he was unable to pass the driver's test. He rode a bike in the good weather and walked in bad weather. He had been an only child. His father had disappeared when jerry was three and his mother had died a few years ago.

Tom gave Jerry a ride home and accepted an invitation to come inside the small house. It was small, but well kept. Jerry might not dress well, but he kept the small house neat and clean. Something Tom had not been able to do when he was in the depths of his depression in Des Moines. Jerry proudly displayed his most prized possession. A big screen television that seemed to take up a whole wall of the small living room.

"I got satellite tv and I get all the college basketball games," said Jerry. "I never miss an Illinois game if it's on tv."

When they were boys and teammates on the Galva High School varsity basketball team, Tom and Jerry had dreamed of playing for the Fighting Illini. Neither one of them was good enough for that level of play. Jerry had gone straight into the army after high school and Tom had gone to college and played as a reserve on a small college team.

When Tom got back to his sister's place, he called Jerry on the phone and asked him to come over the next Saturday and watch Illinois play Wisconsin in a football game. Jerry readily agreed. When Tom hung up the phone he was smiling. Then he remembered to clear it with his sister who laughed and agreed to inviting Jerry over to watch the game.

Soon Tom was including Jerry in his few social outings including trips to Kewanee and Galesburg to see a first run movie. A movie and pizza afterwards were the extent of most of their outings. In November, Tip produced two tickets to the Illinois vs. Arizona basketball game in Champaign. It was a long trip, and they didn't get back to Galva until early in the morning. They had a great time.

As soon as the high school basketball season began, Tom and Jerry went to the home games and Tom drove them both to the away games. Tom got to see his six protégé's play in the sophomore game and they won all but one of their first six games. Tom explained to Jerry who the players were and what nicknames he had given them. After reading his first game program, Tom learned what the real names of the six boys were.

Brick was Wade Nylinger. Pick was Dan Humphrey. Red was Leland Lapan. Swifty was Tony Frank. Lefty was Mike Leff. Lurch was Tim Yocum. Tom found it funny to finally be confronted with the six boys' real names. He decided to stay with the nickname. They were much easier to remember.

Tom felt a sense of pride as he watched the boys play. Their coach was a first-year teacher who had very little basketball experience. He stuck with simple and elementary plays and the six sophomores did very well with little help from their coach.

After the frosh-soph game came the varsity game. The varsity coach was a middle-aged man named Froster Chandler. He had been hired three years ago after being fired from a larger school in upstate Illinois. He was a loud and often profane coach who yelled at his players, his assistant coach, the trainer, the cheerleaders, and whoever was selling popcorn. It wasn't personal with Frosty. He yelled at everyone. Frosty was divorced. He probably yelled at his wife until she got tired of it. Frosty had a large head and a large nose. The nose was heavily veined and to Tom it looked like the man had a fondness for alcohol.

Tip had told Tom the schoolboard was nervous about Frosty. They hired him so they could win basketball games, but they worried about the trouble he might get into. He did have a history of excessive drinking.

Frosty employed a 2-3 zone defense and a 1-3-1 offense. His team had decent players, but they were slow. They were slow to get back on defense and they were slow to spot an open man. They passed the ball too slowly on offense and reached too slowly on defense. They could shoot, but they played poor defense. They scored a lot but were frequently outscored. They had lost more games than they had won going into the December Holiday Tournament. The week before the tournament they won a game over an undermanned Williamstown team.

After the game, Frosty invited the team over to his house to celebrate. He was in a rare, good mood. It was not to last.

CHAPTER FIVE

Tip was waiting at the breakfast table on Sunday morning, two days after the Williamstown game. Beside him the newspaper sat untouched as was the cup of coffee in front of him.

Tom grabbed a cup of coffee and sat down across from Tip. Tip had a look on his face that might be more suited to a formal courtroom setting. Tom braced for what he surely felt must be some sort of bad news.

"Tom, something unpleasant has happened," said Tip.

Tom sipped at his coffee and kept his mouth shut as he waited for Tip to continue.

"Last Friday night the high school basketball coach invited the varsity over to his house to celebrate their win over Williamstown. The party got out of hand and the coach apparently provided alcohol to the players. One of them got into an argument with the coach and the coach punched the player. A neighbor called the police and they arrested everyone at the party. The school board met in emergency session yesterday and the coach was fired, and the players were suspended from school and dismissed from the team," said Tip.

"How do you know all this?" asked Tom.

"I'm the legal counsel for the school district and I attended the meeting," said Tip.

"Oh, I see," responded a surprised Tom.

"The school board decided to offer the coaching job to the frosh-soph coach since his players are now the varsity. He refused unless the board re-wrote his contract. They were willing to do that, but he demanded more money than they were paying Frosty, and they refused to meet his demands," said Tip.

"Why are you telling me about this?" asked a puzzled Tom.

"Because I have been asked by the school board to offer you the job, on an interim basis, of course" said Tip softly.

"Me! Why would they offer me the job?" asked a shocked Tom. "I have no coaching experience. The board doesn't even know who I am."

"They know who you are, Tom. This is a small town. Even the frosh-soph shop coach mentioned the work you had done with six of the sophomores over the summer. Plus, you are a former Galva High player. That counts for a lot with the board, especially after what just happened with Frosty," said Tip.

"I don't think so," said Tom. "I'm not qualified. I'm not a licensed teacher."

"You don't have to be," said Tip. "You are hired as a coach only. Plus, you have my recommendation," replied Tip.

"You don't know anything about me as a coach," said Tom.

"Yes, I do," replied Tip. "We interviewed the frost-soph players and the six boys you coached over the summer asked us to consider you for the job. Look, the board is in a tough spot. The offer is just for an interim job. You can really help them and the town out. The board has done the right thing for the school and the town, and they need a little help."

Tom sat back in his chair. His coffee cup sat on the table in front of him. Then he looked up at Tip. "Let me think about it, Tip. I appreciate your support, but I'm not sure I can manage a job like that," said a shaken Tom.

"Take a couple of days, Tom," replied Tip. "But from what I saw and heard about this summer from those boys, you were born to coach."

Tom excused himself and went out for a walk and some fresh air. Snow had begun to fall and the grass in the park was coated with a dusting of white. So were the branches of the trees, especially the evergreens. As he walked around the perimeter of the park, he thought about what Tip had said. Could he do this? Could he handle the pressure? Could he help these kids? Could he help his old school? By the time he had almost finished his work, he found himself on the edge of the park basketball court. By now snow covered the court and snow hung from the chain links of the nets under the basket rims. Tom thought about all the hours he had spent with the six boys over the summer and how much it had meant to him and how much he had enjoyed it. Maybe Tip was right. Maybe this was what he was meant to do. There was only one way to find out.

Tip was reading the Sunday paper in the living room when Tom walked back into the house. Tip looked up at his snow-covered brother-in-law.

"I'll take the job with one condition," said Tom.

"And that is?" asked Tip.

"I get to hire my own assistant coach," said Tom.

"Is he a teacher at the school?" asked Tip.

"Nope. He's a former Galva High School player," responded Tom.

"You have a deal," said Tip with a huge smile on his face.

They spent a few minutes working out the details including the pay, and then Tom thanked Tip again and ran down to the garage and backed his Jeep out into the snow-covered street.

Five minutes later Tom pulled up in front of a small, but well-kept house. Jerry answered the door. He was dressed in an old long sleeved flannel shirt and tattered jeans.

"What's up, Tommy?' asked a surprised Jerry.

"The High School needs a basketball coach, and they've asked me to do it. I can't do it without a good assistant, and I need you," said Tom.

Jerry paused for a minute. Then he spoke. "Let me get my coat, Tommy Boy. Sounds like we have some work to do," he responded.

THE END

ACKNOWLEDGEMENTS

I hope you enjoyed this collection of short stories. As I mentioned earlier, this is a result of my daughter, Christine Arndt, of Grayslake, Illinois, suggesting I collect all the short stories I have written over the years for distribution to friends and family at Christmas.

I wish to thank my loving and extremely smart wife, Nancy, for all her help in reviewing, correcting, and prodding me in writing this book. As a retired English teacher, she is a godsend for someone as careless as me. I would also like to thank the other folks who take their own time to read and review the proofs of my books including this one. They include Marcia McHaffie, Boulder, CO., Mary Marlin, Longmont, CO., my son Steve Tibaldo, Athens, Alabama, and my fraternity brother, Craig Morrison, Bethel, Connecticut. I recently added a new helper, Julie Radford, Ely, Iowa. Julie is the talented daughter of my first college roommate, Jerry Radford of Solon, Iowa.

I also thank my readers who purchased my books and encourage them to continue to email me with thoughts and suggestions on my books and future projects. As always, I encourage feedback, good and not so good at rwcallis@ aol.com.

Finally, I would like to thank my amazing wife, Nancy Lee Callis, for all the help and support she has given me over the past forty-two years. She passed away on April 16, 2024. I will miss her forever.

Robert W. Callis
Boulder, Colorado

Printed in the United States
by Baker & Taylor Publisher Services